Dear Reader,

Have you ever felt like there are countless rules for being a girl—for being the right kind of girl? *Speak up, but don't be too loud. Be assertive, but not bossy. Be friendly, but don't lead him on.* The rules go on and on.

The pressure on today's girls to be everything—smart, beautiful, poised, funny, fun— is greater than ever. And of course, they should make it look effortless too.

Our protagonist, Marin Lospato, knows the rules by heart, walking this tightrope of contradictions with seeming ease. But when her charismatic young English teacher makes a play for her, Marin wonders if she did something to "ask for it." And when her high school administration shrugs their shoulders at another he said–she said situation, Marin is outraged. She knows what happened—why doesn't anyone believe her? Why doesn't anyone care?

The Rules for Being a Girl was born out of the conversations we've all had with our friends and families—as well as our own personal experiences. When you start to talk about it, you realize stories like Marin's are all too common.

As fans of each other's work, especially the strong female characters we both love, we set out to write a book with a feminist message for our times: We see you. We believe you.

We hope you love this book as much as we loved working on it.

To my sweet, fierce friend Jeanine Pepler

—CB

XOXO
K

CANDACE BUSHNELL

RULES FOR BEING A GIRL

GIRL

NOW SHE KNOWS THEM . . . SHE CAN BREAK THEM

AND KATIE COTUGNO

MACMILLAN CHILDREN'S BOOKS
UNCORRECTED BOUND PROOF

First published in the US 2020 by Balzer + Bray
an imprint of HarperCollins Publishers

First published 2020 by Macmillan Children's Books
an imprint of Pan Macmillan
The Smithson, 6 Briset Street, London, EC1M 5NR
Associated companies throughout the world
www.panmacmillan.com

ISBN 978-1-5290-3608-4

135798642

A CIP catalogue record for this book is available from the British Library.

Typeset by Jenna Stempel-Lobell
Printed and bound by CPI Group (UK) Ltd, Croydon CRO 4YY

To my sweet, fierce friend Jeanine Pepler

—CB

For Baby Girl Colleran, who lived under my heart
while this book got written

—KC

ONE

"And *that*," Mr. Beckett says, leaning against the edge of his desk in third-period AP English, ankles crossed and dark eyes shining, "is the story of how Hemingway and Fitzgerald became the most famous literary frenemies of the twentieth century. Full disclosure, it probably won't be that useful to you on the AP exam, since for some reason they don't test your knowledge of hundred-year-old publishing gossip. But you can keep it in your back pocket and use it to impress your friends at parties." He grins, standing up and tugging a whiteboard marker out of the back pocket of his dark blue khakis.

"Okay," he says, "let's talk homework."

We let out a collective groan, and Bex—which is what we all call him—waves us off as a bunch of bellyachers, then assigns the first forty pages of *A Farewell to Arms* for us to read that night.

"It'll go fast," he promises, twirling the marker between his fingers like a magician with a deck of cards. "One of the great things about Hemingway—and there are a lot of great things about Hemingway, and we'll talk about them tomorrow—is that he's not much for big words."

"Well, that's good," cracks Gray Kendall, a long-legged lacrosse player who just started here back in September. He's sprawled in his chair a couple of rows behind me, a dimple appearing briefly in the apple of his cheek. "Neither am I."

Eventually the bell rings for the end of the period and we all shuffle toward the door, the scrape of chair legs on linoleum and the smell of chicken sandwich day in the cafeteria wafting down the hallway.

"You ready?" I ask Chloe, stopping by her desk at the front of the room. She's wearing her signature red lipstick and huge hipster glasses, her yellow-blond hair falling in soft waves to her shoulders. A tiny lapel pin in the shape of a pink flamingo is affixed to the collar of her uniform blouse.

"Um," she says, glancing over my shoulder at where Bex is erasing the whiteboard, elegant shoulders moving inside his gray cashmere sweater.

I raise my eyebrows at her blatant gawking, and she makes a face at me in return.

"Yeah."

"Uh-huh. Right." I offer her an exaggerated nod and sling my backpack over one shoulder; we're just about to go when Bex looks up.

"Oh, Marin, hey," he says with a guilty shake of his head. "I managed to space on your book *again* today, if you can believe it. But I'll bring it in tomorrow for sure."

"Oh! No worries." I smile.

Bex has been telling me for the better part of two weeks that he's going to lend me his copy of *The Corrections*, which he says I'll love, but he keeps forgetting to bring it in.

"Whenever is good. Honestly, it's not like I have a ton of time to read for pleasure anyway."

"I know, I know." Bex makes a mischievous face. "You're all too busy posting unboxing videos to your YouTube channels, or whatever it is you people do for fun."

My mouth drops open. "Not true!" I say, though my whole body is flushing pleasantly. "Getting buried in AP English homework is more like it."

3

"Yeah, yeah," Bex says, but he's smiling. "Get out of my classroom. I've got lunch duty; I'll see you down there."

"Lucky you," Chloe teases.

"Uh-huh." Bex grins, setting the eraser on the ledge and wiping his hands on the seat of his pants. "You're making fun of me, but joke's on you because you're underestimating how excited I get about chicken sandwich day. Now go."

The cafeteria at Bridgewater Prep is actually a combination auditorium/gym, with a stage at one end and tables that fold down and slide into a storage room during phys ed periods. Ours is already crowded by the time Chloe and I show up, with the same slightly incongruous mix of honors kids from Bex's class and lacrosse bros we've been sitting with since I started dating Jacob.

"Hey, babe," he says now, tweaking me in the side by way of hello. "How's your day?"

"You checking to make sure she's not getting fat?" his buddy Joey cracks, reaching over like he's going to give me a pinch of his own.

I duck out of the way and flip him the finger, rolling my eyes. "Shove it, Joey." Then, nudging Jacob in the shoulder: "Defend my honor, will you?"

"You heard the lady," Jacob says, which is admittedly a little bit weak as far as honor defending goes, but he's pulling

4

me into his lap and pressing a kiss against my cheek, and for a second I forget to be annoyed. Jacob and I have been dating since last spring in AP US History, when we happened to be sitting side by side as Ms. Shah assigned partners for our final research project. I was hoping for somebody who'd let me boss him around and get us both As, which has been my strategy for group projects for basically as long as I've been doing them, but to my surprise Jacob had actual opinions about which primary sources would be most useful to build a document-based question on the social reforms that led up to the Civil War. We argued for two full weeks before we figured out how to work together. When we got our A he lifted me up and twirled me around right there in the middle of class.

Now I sit down in my own chair and pull a turkey sandwich out of my bag, nodding at Dean Shepherd as he sets his tray down beside Chloe. The two of them went to homecoming together earlier this year and since then he's been not at all subtle about trying to date her.

"You going to this thing at Emily Cerato's on Friday?" he asks, cracking the cap on his bottle of Dr Pepper and offering her the first sip.

Chloe shrugs, peeling her clementine industriously. "I was thinking about it," she allows. "You?"

I miss Dean's answer—and, thankfully, most of Joey's ensuing monologue about how hot Emily and her dance team friends all are—catching sight of Bex perched on the stage at the far end of the room, next to Ms. Klein, a bio teacher who was new back in September. She's youngish, in her late twenties maybe, with curly dark hair and glasses and a wardrobe that seems to consist almost entirely of belted shirtdresses from Banana Republic. She's sitting with her ankles crossed inside a pair of boots with blocky wooden heels, eating a cup of fancy yogurt while Bex laughs at something she said.

Chloe flicks a clementine peel at me. "Now look who's gawking," she says, lifting her chin in Bex's direction.

"I am not!" I whisper-yell so Jacob can't hear me.

"Uh-huh. Wipe the drool, why don't you," Chloe says with a laugh.

I sigh dramatically. "I can't help it. You know I'm a sucker for a man in khakis." I glance back at Bex and Ms. Klein. "Do you think there's something going on there?" I'd be lying if I said Chloe and I aren't the tiniest bit obsessed with Bex's romantic life.

"What?" Right away, Chloe shakes her head. "No."

"Why not?" I ask. "Ms. Klein is cute."

"I mean, I guess." Chloe looks unconvinced. "In like, a

local newscaster kind of way."

"I'd nail her," Joey puts in helpfully.

"Nobody *asked* you, Joe." I turn back to Chloe. "I'm just saying: long nights grading papers, romantic looks across the teachers' lounge—"

"Oh my god." Chloe pops a wedge of clementine into her mouth. "Are you sure that isn't *your* fantasy?" she asks. "Maybe you should reconsider becoming a journalist. I feel like romance novels are your true calling."

"This is journalism!" I protest, laughing. "Serious, investigative journalism into the never-before-seen love lives of America's most important national treasure—our teachers."

Chloe snorts. "You do that," she says, tucking her clementine peel back into her brown paper lunch bag. "I gotta go though, I've got a dentist appointment this afternoon, so I'm leaving early. Are you good to run the meeting without me?"

Chloe and I are coeditors of the *Beacon* this year and spend basically every available moment in the office with Bex and the rest of the staff, hunched over the sluggish computers and sprawled out on the ragged, sagging couch.

"Yep, totally. I'll text you tonight." I wave goodbye and turn back to Jacob, who's already finishing his second chicken sandwich. "Do *you* want to go to Emily Cerato's party?" I ask.

"Sure," he says with a shrug, opening a cellophane pack of Oreos. "Why not, right?"

"I don't know." I nibble at a piece of kettle corn. "I was also thinking maybe we could do that movie I was talking about the other day, the one about the sisters who inherit the house?"

"The historical thing?" he asks with a frown. "Wouldn't you rather see that with Chloe or your mom?"

I raise my eyebrows pointedly. "By which you mean you'd rather poke out your own eyeballs than sit through it?"

"I didn't say that," Jacob protests, handing me a cookie in an attempt at a peace offering. "If you want to go we totally can."

"Yeah, yeah." I know he means it too—Jacob's a good sport like that—but there's no point in dragging him to something I know he's going to think is totally girly and boring. "You're off the hook, dude. A party sounds fun."

Jacob nods, then gestures over my shoulder at Bex, who's making the rounds through the cafeteria like a groom at a wedding, coaxing easy smiles out of everybody, from debate nerds to the toughest bruisers on the football team.

"Your boy's coming over here," he tells me. "Should I ask him if he's giving Ms. Klein the D?"

"Oh my *god*," I say, tossing a piece of kettle corn in his direction, "that's disgusting. And also *emphatically* not what I said he was doing." Still, it occurs to me that if Jacob flat out asked Bex if he and Ms. Klein were dating, there's a good chance Bex would tell us the truth. That's one of the nice things about him—he's not obsessed with maintaining some dumb veil of secrecy about his life outside of school, like some of the other teachers. He's an actual human being. Like, the other day in class he told us a story about getting a speeding ticket on the way to school after oversleeping because he was out late at a party in Boston for a friend of his who was publishing a collection of short stories. And on picture day he brought in his own senior yearbook so we could all have a laugh at his mid-aughts puka shells and spiky haircut.

Now he stops at our table for a minute, joking around with Dean and asking Jacob about a play from yesterday's lacrosse game. It's not even lacrosse season, technically, but the Bridgewater team is really good, so they have special permission to play in some indoor intramural league and still use the school buses for games. Everyone thinks the lacrosse guys are something special. Maybe I do too, though frankly it always annoys me that they seem to know it.

"You get your chicken sandwich?" I ask Bex.

Bex nods seriously. "Sure did," he says, then reaches over my shoulder and picks up my bag of kettle corn, helping himself to a handful.

"Excuse you!" I protest, though it's not like I actually mind.

Bex just shrugs. "School tax," he says with a grin. "Take it up with your congressman."

I reach for the bag, but he holds it above my head playfully, laughing at my pathetic attempts to grab it, when we hear Principal DioGuardi clear his throat up on the stage at the far end of the cafeteria.

"Attention, ladies and gentlemen," he says, hands fisted on his hips like a cartoon bodybuilder. Mr. DioGuardi was a PE teacher before he got into administration, and he still kind of looks it, with beefy forearms and a torso shaped like an upside-down triangle inside his maroon button-down. He wears a whistle around his neck, which he uses to keep us from getting too rowdy at assemblies and pep rallies and also sometimes randomly pops into his mouth when he's thinking, like a baby with a pacifier. Last year every single member of the lacrosse team went as him for Halloween.

"If I can have a minute of your time, I wanted to talk

to you about your favorite topic and mine—the uniform code!"

"Oh, Jesus Christ," Bex murmurs, quiet enough that only I can hear him, then gives my shoulder a quick squeeze through my uniform sweater before straightening up and heading back toward the front of the cafeteria. "Here we go."

I look after him in surprise—it's rare to get that kind of unfiltered reaction from a teacher, even one as chill as Bex. Then again, DioGuardi is notoriously ridiculous about the dress code. I've actually never hated wearing a uniform—there's something to be said for not having to worry about picking a cute outfit every day—but lately DioGuardi has been on the warpath, with new rules what feels like every week about everything from skirt length to makeup to how big our earrings can be. Not to mention the fact that the guidelines never seem to apply to the guys.

I glance over at Jacob, but he's scrolling Instagram on his phone under the table, totally unbothered.

"Here we go," I echo, and settle in for the long haul.

That afternoon I'm sitting on the ancient couch in the newspaper room working through a problem set in my calc book when Bex pauses at the open door. It's after five, and our meeting ended a couple hours ago, but I'm stuck waiting for my mom to pick me up. "Hey," he says, glancing at the clock above the whiteboard. "You got a ride?"

"Oh, yeah," I tell him. He's wearing a buttery-looking leather jacket, his dark hair curling over his collar. There's a rumor that Bex paid his way through grad school by modeling—supposedly some senior dug up the pictures online last year, though Chloe and I haven't ever been able to find them ourselves—and right now I can believe it. "My mom'll be here in a while. I mean, I have my license, obviously, but—one car. And my sister has a chess thing." I shrug.

Bex raises his eyebrows. "A chess thing?"

"My little sister is a Massachusetts chess champion," I explain, a little embarrassed. "She gets lessons from this crotchety old guy out in Brookline. Normally my dad would just come get me, but he had a meeting, and Chloe had a dentist appointment, so—" I snap my jaws shut, not sure why I feel compelled to bore him with the mundane logistical details of my life. "Anyway. I'm good."

Bex just smiles. "Come on," he says, nodding in the general direction of the parking lot. "I can drive you."

"Oh." I shake my head like an instinct, pulling the scratchy blue sleeves of my uniform sweater down over my hands. "No, that's okay, you don't have to do that."

Bex shrugs. "I wouldn't offer if I didn't mean it," he says

12

easily. "Pretty soon it's going to be just you and Mr. Lyle rattling around this place."

Mr. Lyle is the janitor, who's seven feet tall and almost as wide in the shoulders. Everybody calls him Hodor behind his back.

"Grab your stuff."

I glance out the window, at the dusk falling purple-blue behind the pine trees. Back at Bex. "Okay," I say finally, swallowing down a thrill and reaching for my backpack. "Sure. Thanks."

I text my mom to let her know I've got a ride and follow Bex down the empty hallway and out into the teachers' lot, explaining where I live as we walk. He drives a beat-up Jeep with a peeling Bernie Sanders sticker on the bumper. Inside it smells like coffee; there's a gym bag slouched on the back seat. As he starts the engine the car fills with sad, guitar-heavy indie folk—Bon Iver, I think, although possibly that's just the only artist like that I could name.

"I'm a caricature of myself, I know," Bex says, nodding at the stereo as we pull out of the parking lot. "All I'm missing is the mountain-man beard."

"No, it's fine," I say with a smile. "I mean, I like to stand outside and weep in the pouring rain as much as the next girl."

Bex lets out a loud laugh. "That's what my ex-girlfriend always used to say," he admits. "She used to call it sad-man dead-dog music."

I laugh too, even as the word *ex-girlfriend* sends a tiny electric shock through me. I wonder what she was like, if she was pretty. Most of all I wonder why they broke up.

Bex has always been strangely easy to talk to for a teacher, and he keeps up a pretty steady conversation as we head for my neighborhood—about DioGuardi and the dress code, yeah, but also about a concert he just went to in Boston and a series of author readings at Harvard Book Store that he thinks I should check out.

"So you and Jacob Reimer, huh?" he asks, turning the music down as we cruise along VFW Parkway, passing the Stop & Shop and the PetSmart. "He seems like a good dude."

"Oh!" I don't know who told him that, and it must show on my face, because Bex mirrors an exaggerated, shocked expression back at me, wide eyes and his mouth a perfect *O*.

"I know stuff," he says, breaking into a grin. "You guys think teachers are, like, deaf, blind dinosaurs, like we shuffle around with no idea what's going on."

"No, that's not what I think!" I protest.

Bex's lips twist. "Yeah, yeah."

"It's not," I insist, giggling a little. "But yeah. Jacob is awesome."

"Good," Bex says, glancing over his shoulder before switching into the turn lane, long fingers hooked casually at the bottom of the wheel. "Most high school guys are basically walking mailboxes. You're right to hold out for someone great."

A pleased, unfamiliar blush creeps up my chest, hot and prickly. I'm glad I'm wearing a scarf. "Thanks," I say, fussing with the sticky zipper on the outside pocket of my backpack, yanking ineffectually at the pull.

Bex shrugs. "It's true."

I nod. "Um, this is me up here," I tell him, nodding at my parents' tiny colonial. "Thanks again for the ride."

"Yeah, no problem."

"See you tomorrow," I say, unlatching the door handle.

"Hey, Marin," he says, laying a hand on my arm as I'm getting out of the car; I feel the zing of it clear down my spine, my whole skeleton jangling pleasantly. "Just to be safe, uh. You probably shouldn't mention to anybody at school that I drove you."

"Oh," I say, surprised. "Okay."

"At the last place I worked it was different—it was a boarding school, so I drove students around all the time, you know? I had students over to my apartment for *dinner* like once a week. But here . . ." He trails off. "DioGuardi runs a different kind of ship."

"No, no, I totally get it." I didn't know he worked at a boarding school before he came to Bridgewater. I'm instantly, weirdly jealous of all the students he ever cooked dinner for. "I won't say anything."

"Thanks, pal," Bex says, grinning a little bashfully. "Have a good night."

"You too," I say, shutting the passenger door gently and lifting my hand in a dopey wave. I stand on the darkened October lawn until the Jeep disappears out of sight.

TWO

Emily's party is two nights later, so Jacob picks me up in the Subaru his parents got him for his seventeenth birthday and we swing by Chloe's house on the way.

"Hey," I say, turning around in my seat as she settles herself in the back, unwinding her fuzzy scarf from around her neck.

Ancient Whitney Houston croons on the stereo, the air in the car heavy with the scent of the cologne Jacob swears he doesn't spray on the heating vents.

"Where were you this afternoon? I thought we were going to do layout stuff."

Chloe shakes her head. "Covered a shift at work," she explains. "Rosie had a doctor's appointment. Sorry, I meant to text you. It was super last-minute."

Chloe's parents own a Greek restaurant called Niko's; we both started working there in eighth grade, first busing tables and now waiting them.

"Bex wasn't there either," I complain, pulling one leg up underneath me and reaching out to turn the heat down. "It was just me and Michael Cyr in there, which meant I had to listen to him talk for like a full hour about how he just discovered *Breaking Bad* and Walter White is his new hero."

"Just you and Michael Cyr, huh?" Jacob asks, glancing over at me from the driver's seat. "Should I be jealous?"

"Only if you feel threatened by a guy who met all his best friends on Reddit," I say, reaching out to poke him in the rib cage.

Jacob grabs my finger and squeezes. Chloe rolls her eyes.

Emily's house is a sprawling ranch in a midcentury development full of identical sprawling ranches, all of them painted in different pastel colors.

"Once, when I was in second grade, I got off the bus and walked right into the wrong one," Emily says, leading us down the hallway and pulling a couple of beers out of an iceless cooler near the back door. "This old lady Gloria sat me down at her kitchen table and made me soda bread, and then she was my best friend for like three years until she died."

Right away Jacob gets absorbed into a crowd of his lacrosse buddies—Joey and Ahmed, plus Gray Kendall and a few other dudes. The rumor is Gray got kicked out of his fancy prep school last year for throwing the kind of wild parties where people wind up in the hospital for eating Tide Pods. In barely two months at Bridgewater he's fooled around with what seems like basically every girl at school, an unending parade of hopeful-looking underclassmen hanging around outside the locker room on game days. It's deeply embarrassing for everyone, although I can admit he's ridiculously cute.

Chloe and I make ourselves comfortable on the staircase that leads to the second floor, listening to Cardi B rapping tinnily from the Bluetooth speaker on the coffee table. A couple of awkward-looking freshman guys cluster around a video on somebody's cell phone. Slutty Deanna Montalto lounges on the sofa next to Trina Meng.

"Did you hear the thing about Deanna and Tyler Ramos in the auditorium?" Chloe asks quietly, running her thumb around the mouth of her beer bottle. "I feel like she's basically the whole reason behind the new dress-code memo."

"Oh my god, the no-more-knee-socks thing?" Emily asks, plunking down on the stair below us with a can of spiked seltzer in one hand. "So dumb."

"*So* dumb," I agree. "Like, explain to me how these delicate, precious boys are supposedly going to be too distracted by our *knees* of all things to get any work done." I stand up and grab Jacob's arm over the banister, pulling him partway out of the scrum of lacrosse bros. "Can I ask you a question?" I say, lacing our fingers together. "How exactly is us wearing tights instead of knee socks going to help you idiots learn better?"

"It's not," Jacob says immediately, his grin wide and wicked. "What it *is* going to interfere with is Charlie Rinaldi's robust side hustle of taking pictures up your skirts in the cafeteria and selling them online."

Joey and Ahmed bust up laughing. Even Chloe cracks a grin.

"You're disgusting," I inform Jacob, smacking him gently on the elbow, but I can't help but let out a laugh of my own.

The only one who isn't laughing is Gray, who's leaning his lanky body against the post at the bottom of the staircase. "Anybody need a beer?" he asks, holding up his empty bottle. He tips it at us in a salute before he turns and walks away.

"That dude is the fucking weirdest," Jacob says once he's gone, slinging a heavy arm around my shoulders. I watch Gray's broad back disappear into the crowd.

The party breaks up early—turns out Emily Cerato's parents didn't know she was having one to begin with and weren't super thrilled when they came home from dinner and a show down in the Theater District and found two dozen teenagers sprawled all over their furniture.

"How the hell did Emily not realize they were seeing a *one-act* play?" Chloe asks as we dash across the lawn to Jacob's car, her scarf flapping behind her in the sharp autumn wind.

"Maybe we should have tried to convince them they were at the wrong house," I shoot back. That cracks her up, which cracks *me* up; by the time we manage to get our seat belts buckled Jacob looks about ready to leave us both on the side of the road altogether. "Take a little pity on your sober driver, here."

"Sorry, sorry," I assure him, still giggling; I'm pretty sure he finds Chloe and me kind of annoying together, though he's too nice to say so. "Let's go."

Turns out all three of us are starving, so we swing through the twenty-four-hour McDonald's for fries and milk shakes before heading over to Chloe's to drop her off.

"See you at work tomorrow?" I ask, turning around in the passenger seat to look at her. Usually the two of us are on the same Saturday schedule, but tonight she shakes her head.

"I'm off tomorrow," she explains, prying her milk shake out of the cupholder and slinging her bag over one narrow shoulder. "I'm spending the weekend at Kyra's."

I frown. "Really?"

Kyra is her slightly younger cousin, who lives in Watertown and is super into her Greek Orthodox youth group. I know her from years of going to Chloe's birthday parties, and she's cool in a straightedge kind of way, but I definitely wouldn't call them super close.

"Why?"

She shrugs. "My parents want us to be friends, I don't know. They're probably hoping she'll teach me to pray in Greek."

"Oh man," I tease. "Good luck, Kyra."

"Yeah, yeah," Chloe rolls her eyes. "Thanks for the ride, Jacob. I'll see you guys Monday."

Once she's inside, Jacob turns to me, his sharp face

familiar in the light from the dashboard. "You need to get home right away?" he asks.

I glance at the clock, hesitating. I've got a little over an hour before my curfew, truthfully, but I also know what he's actually asking, which is whether I want to go park under the copse of trees at the far end of the Bridgewater parking lot and mess around for a while. "Um."

"We don't have to do anything you don't want to do, obviously," Jacob says quickly.

"Gee, thanks." I make a face.

"Oh, come on." Jacob frowns, wounded. "You know what I mean. I'm not trying to be some, like, pressuring douchebag. I just meant—"

"No, I know." I wave a hand to stop him, a little embarrassed. He's right, actually—Jacob's never given me a hard time about the fact that we haven't had sex yet, even though I can tell he's a tiny bit disappointed every time we're getting up to something and I finally stop him. And it's not even that I don't *want* to, necessarily. I meant what I said to Bex the other day—Jacob is great. He's smart. Everybody is always saying how funny he is. He's the assistant coach of his little brother's peewee basketball team, for God's sake. And if sometimes I feel like I'm still kind of waiting for some crazy *zing* of recognition, some feeling of *Oh, it's you*— Well, this is high school, not a Netflix original rom-com. There's no reason to be such a girl about the whole thing.

Finally I sigh, reaching out with one finger and snapping Jacob's seat belt lightly across his chest. "Let's go," I tell him.

Jacob grins.

THREE

Gracie has a chess tournament in Harvard Square the following weekend, so I tag along with my parents to go see her play. The thing about competitive chess is that even at the middle school level—especially at the middle school level—the various matchups are basically more complicated than March Madness seeding, which means that over the years I've spent an awful lot of time sitting around in random auditoriums waiting for it to be my sister's turn to wipe the floor with supposed prodigies from Newton and Andover.

Today the proceedings are even slower than usual; somebody's little brother is kicking the back of my chair periodically, and the dry, forced heat is making me yawn. Gracie sits to my side with her eyes closed and her head tilted back against the red velvet auditorium seat, listening to Christmas music. My phone buzzes with a text from Jacob—a Bitmoji of himself snowboarding, his tongue hanging out like a dog's. I stopped him—again—before things went too far the night of Emily's party, though he didn't actually seem put out about it. He's spending this weekend at his cousin's house in Vermont, so possibly he's too excited about "shredding the mountain"—his words, not mine—to be annoyed about not getting into my pants.

"I'm going to find a coffee shop and do some homework," I finally whisper.

My mom nods. "Don't go too far," she instructs, fishing a ten-dollar bill out of her purse and handing it over. "I'll text you before her match."

In the end I post up at the big Starbucks near the T stop, the windows fogged with the damp chill outside. I pull my laptop out of my backpack and watch the tourists and college kids waiting in line for their coffees, the hipsters with their tattoos and undercuts. Sometimes I think it would be cool to look a little more like them, to try bright pink hair or an eyebrow ring or whatever. Then I imagine the curious looks and snarky comments I know I'd get if

I ever did anything like that at Bridgewater, and it seems safer to just blend in.

"Marin?"

I look up and gasp, almost knocking over my cup at the sight of Bex standing next to my table in jeans and a worn-in hoodie. With his glasses and his coffee cup he looks like a college kid home for the holiday weekend, messenger bag slung over his shoulder and laptop tucked under one arm.

"I thought that was you," he says.

"Oh!" I steady my cup on the table, offering him a smile. "Hi."

"Sorry," he says, "am I traumatizing you right now?" He grins. "I saw my first-grade principal at the pool once, and I don't think I ever really recovered. A nun in a bathing suit, just to burn that image into your mind like it's burned into mine."

I raise my eyebrows. "Nuns are allowed to wear bathing suits?"

"Apparently." Bex shudders, then nods his chin at my computer. "What are you working on?"

I glance down at the screen with gritty eyes, then back at him. "My admission essay for Brown," I admit.

"Really?" He frowns. "Deadline is coming up, right? It's not like you to have put it off this long."

"It's done, honestly," I confess, dumbly pleased that he's been paying close enough attention lately to know what is and isn't like me. "Or, I mean, it's done in that it's a five-paragraph essay with a beginning, a middle, and an end. I just keep noodling on it though. I want it to be absolutely 100 percent."

"Curse of the perfectionist," Bex says with a knowing smile. "Want me to take a look?"

I shake my head. "You don't have to do that."

"No, seriously," he says. "I want to." He sets his own battered MacBook down on the table. "Come on, hand it over."

"What, right now?"

He shrugs. "Do you have a better time?" He sits down in the empty chair across from me, holding his arms out for my laptop. I click my browser shut—probably there's no reason for him to know that I've been procrastinating by trawling *Riverdale* fan fiction—before passing it across the table, wrapping my hands awkwardly around my empty cup.

"Well, I definitely can't *sit* here while you're reading it," I announce barely five seconds later. I get up and stand in line for another latte—unable to help glancing over my shoulder, searching Bex's face while he reads. His eyes are serious behind his tortoiseshell glasses. The weak afternoon sunlight catches the gold in his hair.

A few minutes later, I walk back to the table, chewing my lip.

"This is fantastic," he says before I even sit down.

I manage to stop my hands before they fly to my mouth, but barely. "Really?"

Bex nods. "Honestly, Marin, I've read a lot of admission essays, and I wouldn't say it if it wasn't true. Your writing is, like, super mature."

"Well, thanks." I glance down at my cup, trying not to smile too widely. He's not the first teacher to tell me that; still, coming from Bex it's like it somehow means more. "I mean, realistically I'm still going to be messing with it until the deadline, but I really appreciate it."

Bex laughs. "I'm the same way. Like I said: curse of the perfectionist," he says, tilting his chair back onto its hind legs as if he's sitting in a classroom himself. "Listen, I don't know if you know this, but I went to Brown. And so did my dad . . . and so did his dad, actually." He smiles a little sheepishly. "When you go for your interview, look out for Beckett Auditorium."

"Oh, wow," I say, eyes widening as I cop on. I had heard his family had money, but I never realized there was *that* much of it. "Yeah, I will."

"Anyway, I just wanted to say that if you ever wanted me to put a call in, try and throw my weight around a little bit, I'd be happy to do it. I don't know if anyone there will give a shit, but it couldn't hurt, right?"

"Thank you," I say, nodding my head and mustering a smile. "That would be amazing."

Bex nods, satisfied. "Honestly, my pleasure. You earned it."

"So, um, what about you?" I ask, motioning with my cup at his laptop. "What are you working on?"

"Oh, Jesus," he says with a rueful shake of his head. "You don't want to know."

I raise my eyebrows. "Well, now you have to tell me."

"My novel." Bex visibly cringes, dropping his face into his hands. "I can't believe I'm even saying that out loud to you right now. Go ahead, have a laugh."

My eyes widen. "You're writing a *novel*? Seriously? What's it about?"

Bex sighs theatrically, lifting his head to look at me again. "I'm trusting you with this, you realize. You could ruin me."

"I wouldn't do that."

"No, I know you wouldn't." He shifts his weight again,

the front legs of the chair hitting the tile floor with a clatter. "It's about a guy who wants to be a theater actor, but he's not a very *good* theater actor, so he's working for a children's theater doing puppet shows about the Revolutionary War and stuff. And then his dad dies." He makes a face. "See, it sounds stupid when I say it out loud."

"It doesn't sound stupid," I promise immediately. "Honestly, it sounds good. Is it, like, autobiographical, or . . ."

Bex makes a face, enigmatic. "My dad is alive," is all he says. "Anyway, I've been writing it since undergrad, and I've got a mostly done draft. But I just keep on . . ."

"Noodling?" I supply with a laugh. "Curse of the perfectionist, right?"

"Exactly," he says, tapping his paper cup against mine.

I'm expecting him to move to one of the other empty tables, but instead he stays where he is while I drink my second latte, caffeine buzzing wildly through my veins. We chat about all kinds of things: our Starbucks orders—Americanos, he tells me—and his parents' aging collie, an exhibit on protest art he saw at the contemporary art museum. I'm struck again by that same feeling I had the day he drove me home after school a couple of weeks ago, that he's weirdly easy to talk to for a teacher.

Not just for a teacher. For a *guy*.

I feel a blush creeping up my chest underneath my sweater, glancing over at the baristas behind the counter and wondering idly if they think Bex and I are on a date. And like, obviously *I* don't think we're on a date—he's my teacher, and he's like thirty years old—but as we sit here I can imagine dating someone like him. Someone who cares about what new plays are workshopping in Boston. Someone who knows the name of the Speaker of the House.

I drink my coffee slowly on purpose, both in an attempt to keep Bex talking and because my hands are starting to shake from all the caffeine. Out the window it's beginning to get dark. I know I should probably get back to the tournament, but part of me feels like I could hang out in this Starbucks all night. That's when Bex's phone dings in his pocket.

"Holy sh . . . ," he says when he looks at it, glancing at me and trailing off before completing the swear. "Is it really after four o'clock? How did that happen?"

I shake my head. "I'm sorry," I say, though I'm not really. "I distracted you. You didn't get any writing done."

Bex shrugs. "Let's be real," he admits, "I probably wasn't going to get any writing done anyway." Then he grins. "Besides, the conversation was worth it."

He stands up and slings his messenger bag over his

shoulder, lifts his empty cup in a salute. "Enjoy the rest of the weekend," he says with an easy smile. "And send that admission essay off before you come into my class on Monday. Noodling time is officially over."

"I will," I promise. I watch his back until Bex disappears into the crowd outside.

FOUR

My dad makes a double batch of chicken noodle soup for dinner on Sunday night, so on Monday after school I head over to Sunrise Senior Living to drop a container of it off for Gram. I know most people think nursing homes are totally creepy, and I guess they're not wrong, but I've been coming here for so long at this point that the bleachy smell and occasional confused, wandering person don't really bother me that much.

"I mean," I pointed out to my mom the last time the two of us came to visit together, "depending on your perspective, it's not actually that different from high school."

I check in at reception before climbing the stairs in the atrium and waving hello to Camille, the nurse supervisor on Gram's floor. She's wearing a pair of scrubs printed with wildflowers and a pair of bright green Crocs. Camille has scrubs in a riot of different patterns and Crocs in every color of the rainbow; she's wearing a different combination every time I see her, mixing and matching like she's a walking, talking paper doll.

"Hey, Marin," she says, tilting the plastic tub of cat-shaped Trader Joe's cookies on the counter in my direction. "All those college apps submitted?"

"Yup," I reply, reaching for a cookie. I took Bex's advice and hit send over the weekend, dorkily emboldened by his pep talk. "They're all in."

"And you're going to bring me a T-shirt when you get into Brown, right?"

"A T-shirt, a pennant," I promise her. "One of those big blankets you're supposed to use at football games, maybe."

"See now, you're making fun, but I'm gonna hold you to it." Camille grins. "Go on in, honey."

Gram's door is propped halfway with a doorstop shaped like a Boston terrier, but I knock lightly to give her some warning before easing it all the way open.

"Hey, Gram."

When she first moved in to Sunrise back when I was in middle school, Gram still had way more good days than bad days, starting a little rose garden at the back of the building and organizing pinochle tournaments in the rec room. It's about fifty-fifty now; she always remembers me, but according to my mom and Camille it's better not to startle her.

"There she is!" Gram says with a smile, setting her book—a thick, slightly grisly looking mystery—down on the side table. Gram has been a member of the Book of the Month Club since the seventies, and everybody says I get my book-nerd genes from her. "Come here, you."

I bend down to wrap my arms around her narrow shoulders, careful. Gram's always been thin, but in the last couple of years she's gotten downright fragile. She says it's because she doesn't like the food at Sunrise, so a lot of times Mom and Gracie and I will cook her old recipes—chicken parm, baked ziti, her famous meatballs—and bring them over. Still, she's got to weigh less than one hundred pounds. I remember her swinging me up into the waves when I was a little kid at the beach on the Cape, how strong and tan her shoulders were. These days she feels like a bird in my arms.

"Come sit," she says now, motioning to the chair across from her, a roomy upholstered holdover from her house

36

back in Brockton. Her room at Sunrise is suite-style, with a sitting area, a bedroom alcove, and a private bathroom she's outfitted with fancy hand soap from Williams-Sonoma and a curtain printed with arty pineapples. "Tell me about your day."

"It was okay," I say, sticking the soup in the mini fridge and hooking my backpack on the coatrack. "Pretty uneventful."

"Uneventful!" Gram raises her eyebrows, which she fills in every morning with a dark brown Revlon pencil, before getting up and heading over to the tiny kitchenette at the far end of the sitting room, pulling a jug of iced tea from the mini fridge. "How evocative."

"Sorry, sorry." I smile guiltily. "I guess it was just kind of tough to be back in school after the weekend, that's all."

Gram nods. "You know, people always say that high school is the best part of your life," she says, pouring me some without bothering to ask if I want it or not. "But that's just baloney. You're going to go to college, you're going to find out just how much there is for you out in the world. You'll see."

"I just scheduled my interview for Brown, actually," I tell her, taking a sip of my iced tea. "So with any luck, you'll be right."

"See?" Gram beams. "There you go." She went to Brown herself—or to Pembroke, technically, which is what the women's college was called before the university went coed in the seventies. She took me as her date to her fiftieth reunion a few years back, which is when I decided I wanted to go there myself. I still remember the look in her eyes when I told her, the way her whole face seemed to glow.

Now she reaches up with her free hand, tucks my hair behind my ears. "You're such a good girl, my Marin," she says. "You don't always have to be so good though. Lord knows I wasn't."

"Oh no?" I ask, unable to hide a smile.

"Don't laugh," Gram says. "I'm serious."

"I believe you," I promise, although actually I don't. For all her style and sophistication, Gram is one of the most buttoned-up people I've ever met: she married my grandpa when she was twenty-two, then raised my mom and her brothers while working part-time as a bookkeeper for a discount mattress company and hosting Tupperware parties on the weekends. I've literally never seen her without lipstick; she's been wearing the same shade of Clinique since at least the eighties. "I want to hear more about this wild and crazy past, Gram."

"Oh," she says, waving her hand, the clear polish on her nails catching the sunlight trickling in through the window.

"Oh," she says again, and just like that I know her mind is wandering. The most surprising thing about Gram's illness is how fast it can make itself obvious, like she's walked out of the room even though she's still sitting right here.

"You want to see if Ina is on?" I ask before she can get flustered, reaching for the remote on the coffee table and clicking over to Food Network. My grandmother is obsessed with the Barefoot Contessa; my mom still buys her all the cookbooks on the day they come out, even though she only has a microwave and an electric kettle in her suite. Still, every once in a while we'll come visit on a special occasion and find she's made candied nuts or a specialty cocktail. I suspect Camille has something to do with it.

"She's not on until four," my gram says now, frowning; her voice has taken on a different quality, thinner and a tiny bit peevish. "And I don't like this other woman with all the cattle." Still, she settles in to watch anyway, her knobby fingers wrapped around her glass of iced tea. I lean my head against the back of the chair.

My mom is prepping chicken cutlets for dinner when I get

home from Sunrise late that afternoon, the kitchen warm and cozy even as the early dusk presses against the windows above the sink. The familiar smells of garlic and butter are heavy in the air.

"How was chess?" I ask Gracie, plucking a grape from the bowl on the counter and popping it into my mouth.

"Fine," Gracie says with a shrug. She's sitting at the peninsula, reconnecting my mom's phone to the Bluetooth speaker my dad got her last Mother's Day; no matter how many times Gracie does it for her, my mom always insists it doesn't work. "I won my match."

"She beat the pants off that smug little fish-face Owen Turner," my mom—who has never let anyone's age keep her from declaring them a blood enemy—says gleefully.

I laugh, reaching out and tugging the end of Gracie's ponytail. "Well done."

"Thanks," she says, nodding with satisfaction as the speaker finally connects and the Italian opera music my mom loves fills the kitchen. "He said he was going to have to live the rest of his life in a remote village in Siberia to atone for the shame of losing to a girl."

"Well, fish-face Owen Turner is welcome to do us all a favor and pack his bags," I say brightly.

"That's what I said!" My mom drops a kiss on my temple

as she pulls a tub of frozen tomato sauce out of the freezer and sticks it in the microwave. "How was Gram?" she asks, once she's hit the start button. Her voice is carefully casual, but she can't disguise the flicker of worry across her face.

"She was fine," I say, leaving out that one weird moment where she seemed to lose her train of thought. After all, it's not like there's anything anyone can do about it, and there's no point in worrying my mom for no reason. I open the door to the refrigerator, waggle a bag of lettuce in her direction. "You want me to make a salad?"

My mom looks at me for another moment, eyes just slightly narrowed. Sometimes I think she's psychic when it comes to me lying. "Sure," she says finally. "A salad would be great."

FIVE

Chloe wants to get an early start on her Christmas shopping, so we take the T into the city after school on Thursday to poke through the boutiques on Newbury Street. It's feeling like the holidays for real now, the old-fashioned lampposts festooned with evergreen wreaths and all the store windows lined with twinkle lights and sprayed with fake snow. The dusky sky is a November purple-blue.

"Did you know Bex is writing a novel?" I ask as we wander through the huge Urban Outfitters, pawing through racks of fuzzy sweaters and scented candles. I pick up a giant pair of white plastic sunglasses with heart-shaped lenses and wear them around the store for a while, making dumb faces into every mirror we pass.

Chloe looks at me over a display of coffee-table books. "How do *you* know that?" she asks.

I raise my eyebrows. "So you did know?"

"No," she says, putting down the question-a-day journal she's been considering and turning toward a rack of organic lipstick. "When did he tell you about it?"

"I saw him at Starbucks in Harvard Square over the weekend," I tell her—aware even as I'm saying it that it sounds a little bit like I'm bragging, and there's a tiny chance that maybe I am. "We wound up sitting there and talking for, like, two hours."

Chloe looks surprised. "Seriously?" she asks. "What the heck did you guys even talk about for two hours?"

From the tone in her voice I can't tell which one of us she thinks would have dragged down the conversation, Bex or me.

"I mean, I don't know," I say, suddenly wishing I hadn't told her. "Random stuff, I guess. His novel, for one thing."

I fill her in on the plot points, which actually do sound a tiny bit ridiculous now that I'm the one doing the explaining. "He does a better job talking about it," I promise finally, putting the sunglasses back on the rack.

I'm expecting her to laugh, or at least be really into it, like she was back in September when we spent the full duration of a Harry Potter marathon on cable trying to figure out if he had a secret Instagram, but Chloe only shrugs, winding her scarf around her neck and nodding toward the exit.

"Come on," she says, "let's go. They don't have anything I want here."

"Okay." I follow her out onto the bustling rush-hour sidewalk; it got all-the-way dark while we were shopping, a raw, icy snap in the air. "Who are you shopping for, anyway?" I ask her, tucking my hands in my pockets to warm them.

"Nobody," she says, and forges ahead of me into the crowd.

Chloe's weird mood lingers all through the hipster bookstore and the fancy coffee shop, though she perks up when we wander into the big mall on Boylston Street, her glasses fogging up in the sudden warmth. She leads me up the escalator and directly into Sephora, her expression faintly beatific as she weaves through the rows of mascara and bronzer, picking up my wrist and spritzing me with perfume samples until I cough.

"Thank you for that," I say, sniffling a bit in a slightly suffocating cloud of vanilla and jasmine.

"You're welcome," she replies sweetly, breathing in deeply and setting the bottle back on the shelf. Sephora is Chloe's own personal happy place. "Come on, I need new lip stuff."

"Speaking of lip stuff," I say, following her through the crowded aisles, "you and Dean seem pretty friendly lately."

"Say what now?" She stops in her tracks beside a stack of metallic eye shadow palettes, her face crinkling up like I've lost my mind. "Me and *Dean?*"

"What?" I ask, weirdly put off by her tone—after all, it's not like I'm pulling the idea out of nowhere. He was hanging around her locker literally this morning in an against-dress-code hoodie, munching a family-size bag of trail mix with M&M's. "What's wrong with Dean?"

"I mean, nothing's *wrong* with him," Chloe concedes, shrugging inside her puffy black coat and turning toward the M•A•C display. "And yeah, I guess he's been sniffing around or whatever since homecoming."

"Okay," I tell her. "So?"

"So, nothing." Chloe turns toward the lipsticks.

"Is this about Frank with the Sweatband from the Deli?" I tease. Chloe broke up with Frank with the Sweatband from the Deli back in the summer—which, come to think of it, makes this the longest she's gone without having a boyfriend pretty much since we met. "I mean, sure, he always kind of smelled a *little* like Genoa salami, but I'm not judging. The heart wants what it wants, et cetera."

"Oh my god, he did not!" Chloe smacks me in the shoulder, but she's laughing, which was the whole point. "And no, thank you, this is not about Frank with the Sweatband from the Deli. I don't know. I just kind of feel like I'm over high school boys, that's all."

"Oh yeah?" I say with a snort. "Gonna start trolling the Saint Xavier's parking lot, maybe pick up a sixth grader or two?"

"Wow, you are just on fire over there." Chloe makes a face. "I'm just saying. We'll be in college soon, and then . . ." She trails off, plucking a pot of lip stain off the rack and holding it up to the light. "I don't know," she says again. "Like, do you think you and Jacob will stay together?"

"I—" Haven't thought about it really, but it feels messed-up to say that out loud, even to Chloe. "I guess it depends where we wind up going," I hedge, examining a tube of concealer instead of looking directly at her.

"You mean how close he is to Brown?" she asks with a grin.

"Don't even say it!" I make a face. "We don't know that I'm getting in to Brown."

"*I* know you're getting into Brown," Chloe declares, then holds up two red lipsticks. "Which one?"

I squint. "Those . . . are one hundred percent identical."

Chloe huffs. "They are not!" she protests. "Ugh, they have completely different undertones. You're useless, you know that?"

I hold my hands up like, *What can you do?* "You love me."

"I do," she admits, linking her arm through mine and tugging me toward the checkout. "Come on. I'm getting them both."

SIX

I'm heading for my locker after the last bell on Friday when I pass by the newspaper office and spy Bex lounging cross-legged on the sofa.

"Hey," I say, rapping lightly on the open door.

Bex doesn't have an office, per se, but a lot of times he hides out in here if he's got grading to do and doesn't want to deal with the teachers' lounge.

"Hey," he says now, struggling upright. He's wearing khakis and a blue plaid button-down rolled to his elbows, glasses slipping down his face the slightest bit. "Headed out?"

"Almost," I say, pulling my ponytail down over one shoulder. "Although, actually, if you've got a minute, can I run an idea for an article by you really quick?"

Bex nods, gesturing at the other end of the sofa before pulling a desk chair over to use as a footrest. "By all means."

"Thanks," I say, reaching down and pulling my planner out of my backpack. "Okay, so I was thinking—" I break off suddenly as he lets out a giant yawn, dark eyes squinched shut and the pink flash of his tongue. "Sorry," I say with a laugh, a little embarrassed. "Am I keeping you awake?"

"No, no, no, I'm sorry." Bex shakes his head, taking his glasses off and scrubbing a hand over his face before replacing them. "I just haven't been sleeping much, honestly."

"Uh-oh," I say, a sharp little thrill running through me. The word *sleeping* feels weirdly intimate coming from him, like even mentioning it opens some invisible door to the thought of . . . whatever else people do in beds. "Too many exciting papers to grade?"

"Obviously," Bex replies with a rueful smile. "No, um, honestly? My ex and I have been trying to work it out, and it's just been . . ." He waves a sheepish hand. "Yeah. It's just been."

I blink. "Oh." I keep my voice neutral, like teachers talk to me about their various romantic relationships all the

49

time and he's the fourth or fifth of the week. I really don't want to think about what getting back together with his ex-girlfriend has to do with him not getting a lot of sleep—or, more truthfully, I maybe I do, even if that's totally crossing the line.

"Anyway," Bex continues with a twist of his lips, "we ended it for good last night. Thus"—he gestures down at himself—"the desiccated corpse you see before you today."

I smile. "That sucks."

He shrugs. "It's for the best," he admits. "The thing about Lily is that she's just really—" He breaks off. "I'm sorry. This is literally the last thing I should be talking about right now."

"No, no," I say, totally curious. I can't help it. I pull one leg up underneath me on the sofa. "It's okay."

"I mean, it's not, probably," Bex counters with a shake of his head. "It doesn't exactly win me any points as an authority figure, that's for sure. But I don't know, you just kind of seem, like . . . *older* than other girls in your grade. Has anybody ever told you that?"

Nobody ever has, actually; I think about how I secretly played Littlest Pet Shop until Chloe caught me at it halfway through seventh grade. "I do?"

"Yeah," Bex says, no hesitation at all. "Honestly? I've

taught a lot of teenagers. And I like teenagers, don't get me wrong. But sometimes I listen to what, like, Emily Cerato and her friends are talking about in my classroom, and I think . . . Marin's not like that. It's like you've got an old soul or something."

Pleasure blooms inside my chest, huge and sudden. "Well," I say, ducking my head down and smiling at my planner. "Thanks." When I look up again, Bex is smiling back.

We stay there for the better part of an hour, him grading and me working on a set of calc equations that aren't due until halfway through next week. It's after four when Bex finally stands up and stretches, his shirt coming a little bit untucked, so I can see a flash of smooth bare skin at his hip.

"Okay," he says, stifling another yawn with a guilty smile. "Time to get out of here, Lospato. You need a ride home?"

"Oh!" It's the first time he's offered since that day a few weeks ago, when he told me not to tell anybody. And I didn't tell anyone, not even Chloe, and maybe there's a part of me that's been holding my breath, waiting for him to ask again. "That'd be great, actually. Thanks."

Bex nods, and I grab my stuff before following him out the side door and across the mostly empty parking lot, both of us squinting in the white winter light. The weather report keeps threatening snow.

"Shoot," Bex says as he's digging his keys out of his messenger bag, smacking the palm of his hand lightly against the hood of the Jeep. "You know what I didn't bring you *again* today?"

"Uh-oh," I say with a laugh. "Let me guess."

"I don't know what's wrong with me," he mutters, buckling his seat belt and turning up the heat. "I mean, sleep deprivation, for one, but that freakin' book has been sitting on my hall table since Halloween, and literally every morning I think, *Don't forget to bring that to Marin*. And every morning I walk out of the house without it."

"Sounds like you should write yourself a Post-it," I tease him.

"If I thought Post-its were enough to get my life in order I'd literally buy stock in 3M," Bex says with a grimace. Then a thought seems to occur to him.

"Actually," he continues as we pull out of the parking lot, "are you in a hurry to get home right now? We could go pick it up on the way."

That surprises me. "You don't have to do that," I say cautiously. On one hand it's not like I'm not curious about where he lives—I'm *super* curious, actually—but on the other I don't want to be a pain in the ass. "You can just bring it to me on Monday, right?"

He stops at a traffic light, fixing me with a dubious look. "Monday, possibly next week. Or next year. Maybe the year after."

"I mean, point taken," I say with a laugh. "Let's go."

Bex lives in a romantically dilapidated Victorian house carved up into three or four apartments. When we pull up to the curb he tilts his head toward the front walk. "Come on in," he says, turning off the engine. "It's freezing out here."

"Oh!" I was fully expecting to wait in the car, peering up at the mismatched windows and trying to figure out which one belonged to him; the thought of seeing the actual inside of his apartment has my heart doing backflips inside my chest. There's a part of me that wants to text Chloe right this second. Another part of me never wants to tell her at all. "Um, okay."

The hallway inside the house is overwarm and violently wallpapered, cabbage roses in aggressive pinks and fuchsias. A dusty chandelier casts dim, dramatic light across his face.

"Watch yourself," he says as I follow him up the staircase, nodding at a place where the maroon carpet is peeling up off the tread. "My mom won't even come visit me here anymore.

She thinks she's going to break her leg or get lead poisoning or something. She sends me real estate listings for these renovated, dorm-looking condos like every single day."

"Aw," I say. An image has started to form in my head of Bex's parents: stern and mostly humorless, the kind of classic New England WASPs we read about in *The Wapshot Chronicle* at the beginning of the year. I feel like he's probably lonely in a family like that. "I think it's great."

As promised, the Franzen book is sitting on the table in Bex's tiny foyer. He hands it over, and I tuck it into my backpack, but instead of herding me back out onto the sidewalk like I'm expecting, he slings his messenger bag over a teetering coatrack and shrugs out of his jacket.

"You hungry?" he asks, putting a hand on my shoulder for the briefest of moments before heading toward the narrow kitchen. "I'm just gonna grab something to drink before we go."

I shake my head. "I'm okay," I say, letting a tiny breath out as I hear him open the refrigerator. I don't want him to catch me gawking, but I can't stop looking around, wanting to commit all of it to memory: the worn leather sofa and the antique desk strewn with papers, the shelves and shelves of books. He's got actual art on his walls—real paintings by actual artists, nothing like the scrolly *Live Laugh Love* canvases my mom is always buying at HomeGoods and hanging on every available surface. A wine crate full of records sits next to a turntable by the window.

I creep farther into the living room, pulling an album out of the pile and turning it over: *Nina Simone Sings the Blues*. The sleeve has gone slightly fuzzy around the corners from being handled. I don't know anything about her, but I make a mental note to google her so I can drop her into conversation later on.

"Whatcha looking at?" Bex asks, coming into the room behind me and peering over my shoulder, a bottle of flavored fizzy water in one hand. His whole house smells like him, coffee and something that might be incense; there are more books stacked in the fireplace, a basket of *New Yorker*s overflowing on the hearth.

I hold up the record, turning to face him. "Do you actually listen to these?" I ask.

Bex smirks. "Yeah, smarty-pants," he says. "Sound quality is way better than Spotify or whatever."

"Is that true?" I ask. "Or is it just, like, what they tell you at Urban Outfitters to make you spend more money?"

Bex's eyes widen. "I don't get my records at Urban fuckin' Outfitters," he says with a laugh, reaching out and taking the album gently from my hand.

"Oh no?" I ask, thrilled and a tiny bit horrified by his language.

Bex grins, a flash of perfectly straight teeth. "No," he says, lacing his fingers through mine and tugging me a step closer to him. "I get them at a record store, like a person with half an ounce of self-respect."

I make a quiet sound then, not quite a laugh, startled by the contact and the movement and the sudden suspicion that something bad is about to happen. He reaches out and pushes a loose strand of hair away from my face.

I don't have time to register any of it though, because that's when Bex puts his free hand on my cheek, ducks his head, and kisses me.

My brain shorts out for a second, lights flickering during a thunderstorm. It's like his mouth is pressed to someone else's, not mine. I stand there frozen and let him do it in the moment, until I feel his hand move down from my face toward my chest. Suddenly every panic response in my body comes screaming to life.

"Um," I yelp, pulling away and taking an instinctive step backward. My neck feels like it's on fire. My skin is two sizes too small. "What are you doing?"

"Easy," Bex says immediately—holding his hands up in surrender, a half smile playing across his face. "I thought you—" He breaks off, clearing his throat. "Easy."

"Um," I say again, taking another step toward the doorway. I remember my mom once describing going out to dive bars in her twenties, how at the end of the night the bartender would suddenly shut off the music and turn the lights all the way up, the fun abruptly over and the whole world in stark relief. "No, I just—I should probably go."

"Oh! Yeah, totally," Bex says. He pats his pockets, flustered. "Lemme just grab my keys and I can—"

"You know what?" I shake my head. "It's not too far from here. I can totally walk."

Bex frowns. "Marin," he says. "Hey. Can we just talk for a—"

"That's okay," I say, my voice canary-bright and maybe a little hysterical. "We're totally good, I swear." I gesture toward the doorway. "I should. Um. Enjoy your weekend!"

I thunder down the narrow stairs and hoof it all the way home, even though it's freezing—my hands jammed in my pockets and a cold wind slicing through my coat. My mom is in the kitchen when I get inside, gathering ingredients for a winter spice cake to bring to my gram while Gracie plays chess on her laptop at the kitchen table.

"Hey," she says, setting the bag of flour on the counter. "I was wondering what happened to you." She looks at me for a moment, eyes narrowing like possibly she can see the blood moving under my skin. "What's wrong?"

I hesitate for a moment, gaze flicking back and forth between my mom and my sister. I have no idea what to say. If I'm being honest with myself, there's always been a tiny part of me that wondered if maybe some of the stuff Bex said wasn't totally aboveboard, if a teacher that chill and funny—and, okay, hot—was too good to be true. If sometimes his attention didn't feel . . . different. But I said yes to the ride anyway, didn't I? I sat with him in the newspaper office.

I agreed to go over to his house.

I mean, what did I *think* was going to happen?

"Nothing," I say now, clenching my fists around the straps of my backpack, then turn on my heels and head upstairs. I shut my bedroom door behind me, digging my phone out of my pocket and scrolling to Chloe's name before realizing I have no idea what to tell her. God, there's probably not even anything *to* tell. I'm blowing this way out of proportion, most likely. Maybe it's not even that big of a deal. After all, it's not like some creepy perv forced himself on me in a dark, deserted alley. It's Bex.

It's *Bex*.

And he *kissed* me.

And maybe I wanted him to, in a way? Except also, I didn't.

I'm still clutching my phone like a weapon when suddenly it buzzes in my hand, startling me so badly I drop it altogether, watching it skitter across the carpet like it's got a mind of its own. I reach down and pick it up, then drop it *again* before finally getting a grip, Jacob's name flashing across the screen. We're supposed to meet a bunch of people at Applebee's tonight, I remember as I hit the button to answer. I'm supposed to go hang out with all our friends.

"Um, hey," I manage, hoping I'm just imagining how fake and squeaky my voice sounds. "How was your practice?"

"It was awesome," Jacob tells me cheerfully, then launches into a long, convoluted story about Joey and Ahmed getting into a fight over whose gym socks were stinking up the locker room that meanders for the better part of five minutes. He's calling from his car, the blare of the radio audible in the background.

"What about you, huh, babe?" he asks finally. "What are you up to?"

"Um," I stall, making a million infinitesimal calculations in the space of a couple of seconds. I can picture him so clearly, his hand slung casually over the steering wheel and everything in his life exactly the same as it was two hours ago. "Not much. Just hanging out."

"You sure?" Jacob asks. "You sound weird."

"I do?" I don't know what it means that I'm surprised that he noticed. "Just tired, I guess."

I can't decide if I'm hoping he'll press it or not, but Jacob just hums along, as usual.

"Take a nap," he suggests cheerfully. "I'm gonna go home and take a shower and then I'll come pick you up for dinner, okay?"

I glance across my bedroom, catching sight of my own reflection in the full-length mirror on the back of the door—my braid and my uniform, the slightly wild expression on my face.

"Sure," I say, looking away again. "Sounds great."

SEVEN

"Okay," I say to Chloe the following night, holding my hand out for the bag of Tostitos she's holding. She came over to my house after our lunch shift at her parents' restaurant, the two of us sprawled out on the floor in my room. "Can I tell you something weird that happened?"

Chloe bites the corner off one triangle-shaped chip, delicate. "Literally always."

"No, I know," I say, rummaging through the bag until I've gathered a salty handful. "This is really weird though, not like, 'Jacob watching those pimple-popping videos' weird."

"Oh, I don't know," Chloe says thoughtfully, "I think those videos are kind of relaxing."

"Oh my god!" I drop my chips back into the bag. "Ugh, you're so gross."

"They are!" Chloe grins. "Okay, okay, go, tell me the weird thing."

I nod, taking a deep breath and telling myself there's no reason to be nervous—after all, it's just Chloe. "Okay," I say again. "So Bex offered to give me a ride home after school yesterday."

Chloe's eyes widen. "He *did*?"

"Yeah," I say, "but that's not the weird part. Or I mean, I guess that's part of what's weird, now that I'm saying it out loud, but—" I tilt my head back against the edge of the bed and tell her the rest of the story, ending with the kiss. "I bailed out super hard right after that, obviously. But now I don't know, like, what to do about it."

Chloe doesn't say anything for a moment. When I look over at her she's breaking a tortilla chip up into a hundred little pieces, arranging them in her lap like a mosaic. "Are you sure?" she finally asks.

I frown. "What do you mean, am I sure? Like, about what happened? Yes, I'm sure. I was there."

"No, I know, I just mean—" She stops. "Like, are you

sure he was actually trying to—like, you didn't just walk into him, or whatever?"

"Yes, I'm sure," I snap, although suddenly there's a tiny part of me that isn't. I sit up a little straighter. "Do you think I'm making it up?"

"Of course not," Chloe says, gathering the chip crumbs up off her lap and tossing them into the wastebasket tucked under my desk.

"Really?" I ask. "Because it sounds like maybe—"

"Marin!" Chloe laughs a little then. "Come on. Hey. It's me. That's not what I think."

"But?" I prompt.

"No buts!" Chloe promises. "That's awful, if he did that. That's totally gross. Was there like—" She breaks off.

"Was there what?"

"I mean, what exactly happened?" she asks, pulling her knees up to her chest and wrapping her arms around them. "Like, was it just a grandma kiss? Was there tongue? What?"

I think of his hand on my face, his palm sliding southward. It feels like somehow I'm not explaining this right. "No," I admit finally. "No tongue."

"Okay," Chloe says, sounding relieved. "Well, that's something, at least."

"I guess." I blow a breath out. "I'm sorry. I'm

just—yeah." I spin around on the carpet, lying back on the floor. "Do you think I should tell somebody?" I ask the ceiling.

"You just told me."

"No, like, DioGuardi or someone? I mean, I didn't even tell my parents."

"What," Chloe asks, "to, like, try to get him in trouble?"

"I'm not trying to get anyone in trouble," I say, popping up on my elbows.

"No, of course not," she says quickly. "I didn't mean that how it came out. I guess I just . . . obviously I believe you about what happened, but are you sure he didn't just, like . . . get confused by your vibe, or whatever?"

I startle. "My *vibe*?"

"You know what I mean!" Chloe defends herself. "Or maybe *you* were confused? I'm definitely not saying you were, I'm just trying to figure out—"

"I'm not confused." Ugh, this isn't going how I thought it would at all. I take a deep breath, try to regroup. "It was weird behavior, right? Objectively, for a teacher? It was inappropriate."

"Yes, of course. One hundred percent," Chloe says, even as she's shrugging noncommittally. "But it also sounds a little like maybe you're freaking out a disproportionate amount? I wasn't there, obviously, but, how many times have we talked about how hot he is, or whatever? Maybe he was just picking up what you were putting down, or trying to make it not weird, or—"

"Seriously?" I interrupt. "How does *kissing* me make it less weird?"

"I don't know!" she says. "I'm just trying to make sense of it, that's all. And if you feel like you need to, like, go to the authorities or whatever, then I'm not going to tell you not to."

"But *you* wouldn't," I say, flopping back onto the carpet.

"I mean, no," Chloe says quietly. "I wouldn't try to ruin somebody's whole life over something I wasn't even sure I interpreted correctly."

"I'm not out to ruin anyone's life!"

"Of course not," Chloe says. "But that's what would happen, right?" She shrugs again. "You tell DioGuardi, and they fire him or whatever, and then he can't get another job because he's got this thing on his record that maybe wasn't even . . ." She trails off, reaching out and balancing a tortilla chip on my knee. "I don't know. It's *Bex*, Marin. He's literally your favorite teacher."

And mine, I can hear her adding in her mind. And everyone's.

"It's not like we have a totally normal relationship with

him anyway," she says.

"Yeah," I say, closing my eyes for a moment. I don't know why all of a sudden I feel like I might be about to cry. "I guess you're right."

For a long time neither one of us says anything. Finally Chloe rolls up the bag of chips. "I've gotta go," she says, reaching for the plastic clip on my nightstand. "I told my mom I'd have the car back by eleven."

She gets to her feet before offering a hand to help me up, the two of us heading downstairs and past my parents watching an old Tom Hanks movie in the living room. "Have a good night, Mr. and Mrs. Lospato!" she calls brightly, pulling her jacket off the overloaded hook in the foyer before turning to me one more time.

"He really did all that stuff?" she asks now, and her voice is very quiet.

"Yeah," I say, still swallowing down that crying feeling one more time. God, how could I have been so stupid? "He did."

Chloe nods, and for a moment it looks like she's going to say something else, but in the end she just reaches out and unlocks the deadbolt, icy December air slicing into the house. "I'll see you Monday," she promises, and just like that she's gone.

EIGHT

I spend the rest of the weekend helping my parents get the Christmas decorations out of the attic and watching *Home Alone* on cable, trying with extremely limited success not to think about what happened. By the time third period rolls around on Monday morning, I'm a nervous wreck. For a minute I honestly consider skipping English altogether, but that's ridiculous, isn't it? What am I going to do, just cut every day for the rest of the year?

Bex isn't in his classroom as we're filing in, and for a moment I wonder—with a mixture of hope and deep, horrifying dread—if maybe he isn't even here today. Did somebody find out what happened between us? Did Chloe turn around and tell? I'm about to hiss her name across the room when Bex ambles in and shuts the door behind him, raising a hand to say hello.

"Sorry I'm late," he says, dimple popping in his cheek as he slings his messenger bag over the back of his chair. "Vending machine in the cafeteria is eating dollars today, just FYI. Not that I was just in there trying to make breakfast out of some barbecue chips and a KIND bar or anything."

He launches into a detailed biography of Joseph Heller, because we're supposed to start *Catch-22* this week. I feel like someone hit me over the head. I don't know what I was expecting, but it wasn't this bland, aggressive normalcy; for one disorienting moment it occurs to me to wonder if maybe I really did make the entire thing up.

Then I remember the press of his mouth on mine, and shiver inside my uniform blouse.

"First forty pages for tomorrow," he calls as the bell finally rings for the end of the period.

I'm shoving my notes into my backpack when he catches my eye from the front of the room.

"Hey, Marin," he says, the very theology of casual, "stick around for a sec, will you?"

So we *are* acknowledging what happened, then. Right

away my skin prickles tightly and my face is on fire. I nod, hanging back as everyone else heads out into the hallway, ignoring the look I can feel Chloe shooting me as she makes for the door.

"So hey," Bex says once we're alone, perching on the edge of his desk and scrubbing a hand over his clean-shaven face. "I feel like we should probably talk, yeah?"

"Um," I say, pulling the sleeves of my uniform sweater down over my hands and crossing my arms like an instinct, shifting my weight in my beat-up Sperrys. "I mean—yeah, I don't know if—"

Bex smiles. "Marin," he says, holding his hands up. "It's just me, okay? You don't have to be afraid of me, or stand here looking like you wish you were dead, or anything like that." He rubs his cheek again, looking sheepish. "Obviously, I . . ." He trails off. "We just . . . I think maybe we had a little bit of confusion there, that's all."

I blink. "Confusion?" I repeat, before I can stop myself.

"Bad communication," Bex continues with a shake of his head. "Mortifying for both of us, obviously. But it happens."

"Um." I swallow. "Sure. Yeah." On one hand, there's something reassuring about the way he's talking about this, like it's just a dumb, awkward thing that happened and not the end of the breathing world. On the other, it occurs to me that he hasn't actually apologized for doing it.

But maybe he doesn't owe me an apology?

After all: *I went to his house. I flirted with him. It's not like I hadn't thought about it before.*

"In any event," Bex says now, sliding off the edge of the desk and heading for the doorway, "I just wanted to clear the air and make sure we can both move on without any weirdness. Honestly, you're such a great student, and I'd hate for this to get in the way of whatever amazing thing you're going to do when you get out of this place." He holds his hand out, like we're about to finish a business meeting. "So. We cool?"

"I—yeah, of course," I say as we shake, the touch of his smooth, cool palm sending a fresh wave of ickiness through me. "We're cool."

NINE

Chloe's waiting for me at our usual spot in the cafeteria, her untouched tray sitting on the table in front of her. "What did Bex want?" she asks, as soon as I sit down.

I shrug. "Just to make sure everything was good, I guess. Like, after—" I glance around. "After."

Chloe nods. "And you told him it was?"

"I mean, yeah." I pull a baggie of grapes out of my lunch bag, plucking them all off the stem at once to avoid looking at her. "What else was I going to say, right?"

Chloe frowns, her signature red lipstick slicked neatly across her mouth. "So it's not?" she asks. "Good, I mean?"

"No, it's not that, I just—" I break off. It's . . . confusing. After all, Chloe and I have been obsessed with Bex for the better part of the school year. But people get crushes on their hot teachers, right? That's a thing that happens. It doesn't mean I wanted—that I was *inviting*—anything real to actually happen between us.

Right?

I'm still trying to figure out how to answer when Jacob and a couple of his lacrosse buddies sit down at the table, their trays heaped with mac and cheese so gloppy you could use it to lay bricks.

"Ladies," he says, and I grin. "What's up?"

"Just talking about newspaper stuff," I say, shooting Chloe a look across the table. "We've got a print deadline at the end of the week." I pop a grape into my mouth. "Actually, did you get those article pitches I texted you?"

Chloe nods, noncommittal. "I had a bunch of ideas too," she tells me. Then, nodding at the mac and cheese on Jacob's tray: "Do you want to write something about the new menu, maybe?"

I laugh out loud, I can't help it.

"What?" She shrugs.

"It's not exactly hard-hitting journalism, that's all."

Chloe frowns again. "Is that what you want to be doing

now?" she asks. "Hard-hitting journalism?"

"I just—" I break off, not entirely sure why she seems so testy all of a sudden. "Isn't that always what we're trying to do?"

Chloe makes a face at that. "I mean, it's a high school paper, Marin," she reminds me. "Not the *Globe* Spotlight team."

I'm starting to reply when there's a commotion up at the front of the cafeteria—it's Principal DioGuardi yet again, a miserable-looking Deanna Montalto in tow.

"Attention please!" he yells out across the room. "Since apparently some of you ladies have still not gotten the memo about the new uniform guidelines, I thought I'd have my friend Deanna here help me show you all what you should not be doing!"

"Seriously?" I look from Deanna to Chloe and back again. "Is he really about to make an example of her right now in front of everyone?"

"Looks that way," Chloe murmurs, biting her lip.

DioGuardi paces back and forth at the front of the cafeteria like a basketball coach watching a scrimmage. "Now," he begins, "who can tell me how Deanna is violating the uniform code today?" He nods at a freshman girl sitting at a table by the window. "How about you?"

"Um," the freshman says, her small voice barely carrying. "She isn't wearing tights?"

"She isn't wearing tights!" DioGuardi echoes cheerfully. "That's certainly one of the problems here. What else?"

Deanna stands silently as DioGuardi points out all her uniform violations one by one, from her untucked shirt to the too-big hoop earrings she's wearing. He even has Ms. Lynch, the school secretary, bring him a ruler so he can measure the length of her skirt.

"This is awful," I mutter, though when I look over at Jacob for confirmation I realize he's watching the proceedings with a good-natured smirk on his face.

"What are you doing?" I ask, jabbing him in the ribs harder than I necessarily mean to. "This isn't funny."

"Aw," Jacob says with a shrug, "it's a little funny. Besides, Deanna doesn't care. A whole cafeteria full of dudes looking at her at once is probably her dream."

"You're being freaking gross," I tell him, even as his buddies bust up laughing. I look back at Deanna's vacant face. I don't know that I've ever sat back and thought super hard about *why* everyone says she's a slut in the first place beyond the fact that her boobs are big and she had a boyfriend back in seventh grade. Even if she *has* been with a million guys, I think suddenly, even if she *is* dressing to get attention, how is that anybody's business but hers?

"Ms. Montalto," Mr. DioGuardi finishes finally, "I will see you in detention this afternoon. As for the rest of you ladies, please remember to dress yourselves in a way that's befitting of the values we uphold here at Bridgewater."

"Yeah, ladies," Jacob teases. "Have some values, why don't you?"

"I can count three different uniform violations on you right now without even trying," I point out. "You're lucky DioGuardi didn't drag you up to the front of the cafeteria in front of everyone."

"Eh." Jacob shrugs, unconcerned. I glance over at Chloe for backup, but she's fussing with her phone inside her bag.

"Can I eat these?" Jacob asks, pointing to the rest of my grapes, and I hand them over without protest. Suddenly I'm not hungry at all.

TEN

That night I sit at my desk eating all the pink Starbursts out of a giant bag I picked up at CVS and staring at the blinking cursor on the screen of my laptop, trying with extremely limited success to put together a draft of this article about the new cafeteria menu. Normally I really like writing for the *Beacon*, but now it feels all mixed up with what happened with Bex, all those afternoons we spent in the newspaper office supposedly having such a good time. I mean, we *were* having a good time. At least I was. But now . . .

Also, damn if it isn't a tall order to make grilled chicken on top of limp romaine lettuce sound exciting and novel.

Finally I push my chair back from my desk, catching sight of myself in the mirror on the back of my closet door. My hair has gotten long, the ends still bearing traces of last summer's sun-and-lemon-juice highlights. When I was little I wanted to look like a mermaid—I remember how Chloe and I used to sleep in braids the night before a beach trip, then hole up in her bathroom or mine slathering on self-tanner, spending way longer getting ready than we ever did messing around in the waves. All at once it occurs to me how much time I've wasted in my life trying to make it look like I haven't spent any at all.

I stand up and face myself full-on in the mirror, taking in my cropped shirt and the sliver of belly that peeks up over my high-waisted jeans and wondering briefly what I'd think if I was a stranger and saw a picture of myself on Instagram. What would I say to Chloe about that girl's flat butt and smudgy mascara? Probably not "She looks smart and like a good friend," that's for sure.

I glance over at the empty place on the carpet where Chloe sat the other night, our conversation replaying like some bad radio earworm inside my head: *You're freaking out a disproportionate amount.* I got so amped up at the thought of it, but what if she's right? I went to his house, I remind myself again. I reapplied my ChapStick right there in his front seat. But was that an invitation? I didn't mean it that way—at least, I don't think I did—but maybe we did just have *bad communication*.

And then I remember: *it happened*. I was there. God, it's like even *I* want to make myself doubt myself. How messed up is that? But there are so many unspoken rules for navigating high school—for navigating life, maybe—that I can't help but try to figure out which one I broke to get myself into this situation. There are so many rules for girls.

I stretch my arms over my head and think again about what happened to Deanna at lunch today, the caught-animal look in her eyes as DioGuardi called her out in front of everyone. The longer I think about it the angrier I get—at DioGuardi, sure, but also at myself. I want to tell Deanna I'm sorry for all the casually nasty, sexist stuff I've ever heard about her, for all the times I could have said *That's not funny* and didn't. I want to tell her how unfair the whole thing is. Like, every guy wants to hook up, but if you actually do hook up, you have to worry about *this*? I want to ask her if she also feels like there are all these guidelines we're supposed to be following in exchange for the alleged privilege of walking around this world as a teenage girl: Be flirty but not *too* flirty. Be confident but not aggressive. Be funny but in a low-key, quiet way. Eat cheeseburgers, but don't get fat. Be chill, but don't lose control. I feel like I could keep on going, like a full list would cover one of those old-fashioned scrolls from cartoons about Santa Claus.

I dig through the bag and unwrap another Starburst, chewing thoughtfully for a moment before laying my hands back down on the keyboard.

THE RULES FOR BEING A GIRL

I type frantically for the better part of an hour, my fingers flying over the keys and my tongue caught between my teeth. I'm just finishing up when Gracie knocks on the door. "Are you going to come watch TV?" she asks, leaning against the jamb in her buffalo-check pajama pants and fuzzy slippers. "Dad's making popcorn."

"I— What?" I feel wrung out like a washcloth; I glance at the clock in the corner of the screen, sure that hours have passed and it's the middle of the night, but to my dazed surprise it's barely nine o'clock. "Um. Sure."

"Okay." Gracie looks at me for another minute. "Are you all right?"

I glance at my editorial, back at my sister. "I'm good," I tell her, smiling a little. And for the first time since that day in Bex's apartment, it actually feels like the truth.

THE RULES FOR BEING A GIRL
BY MARIN LOSPATO

It starts before you can remember: you learn, as surely as you learn to walk and talk, the rules for being a girl. You are Princess. You are Daddy's Little Girl. Are you ticklish? Give him a hug. You're sweet, aren't you? You're a good little girl.

You don't remember those early days, but here's what you do remember: You remember ballet class, the way your tummy stretched your pink leotard and your parents fretted over some future eating disorder, and then you were trying tap, or soccer, or what about a musical instrument? You remember "We just want you to be happy!" and you remember you said you were happy because you knew that's what they wanted to hear. How long have you been saying what everyone else wants to hear?

Time went on, and GIRLS CAN DO ANYTHING! So speak up, I can't hear you! But also: Manners, young lady. A boy is bothering you at school? Stand up for yourself! A boy is bothering you at school? He's just trying to get your attention. Do you like sparkles and unicorns and everything pink? Oh that's stupid now. Can you play in this game? Sorry, no girls allowed.

Put a little color on your face. Shave your legs. Don't wear too much makeup. Don't wear short skirts. Don't distract the boys by wearing bodysuits or spaghetti straps or knee socks. Don't distract the boys by having a body. Don't distract the boys.

Don't be one of those girls who can't eat pizza. You're getting the milk shake too? Whoa. Have you gained weight? Don't get so skinny your curves disappear. Don't get so curvy you aren't skinny. Don't take up too much space. It's just about your health.

Be funny, but don't hog the spotlight. Be smart, but you have a lot to learn. Don't be a doormat, but God, don't be bossy. Be chill. Be easygoing. Act like one of the guys. Don't actually act like one of the guys. Be a feminist. Support the sisterhood. Wait, are you, like, gay? Maybe kiss a girl if he's watching though—that's hot. Put on a show. Don't even think about putting on a show, that's nasty.

Don't be easy. Don't give it up. Don't be a prude. Don't be cold. Don't put him in the friend zone. Don't act desperate. Don't let things go too far. Don't give him the wrong idea. Don't blame him for trying. Don't walk alone at night. But calm down! Don't worry so much. Smile!

Remember, girl: It's the best time in the history of the world to be you. You can do anything! You can do everything! You can be whatever you want to be!

Just as long as you follow the rules.

ELEVEN

I'm headed for my locker the following morning when someone calls my name from down the hallway; I turn, and there's Bex poking his head out of the newspaper room, the collar of his plaid flannel button-down just slightly askew.

"Hey," he says cheerfully, gesturing me over. "You got a minute?"

"Um," I say, glancing at the ancient clock in the hall-way. A week ago I wouldn't have thought twice about being alone in the newspaper room with Bex—would have welcomed it, even, the chance to have his whole and undivided attention—but it isn't a week ago. "Sure."

Bex nods and heads back inside the office, perching on the edge of the desk, but I hover awkwardly in the open doorway, crossing and uncrossing my arms.

"So," he says, in that same cheery voice—and am I imagining it, or does it sound just the tiniest bit hollow? "I just wanted to chat really quick about the editorial you uploaded last night."

"Sure," I repeat cautiously. The essay was the last thing I thought about before I fell asleep and the first thing I thought about when I woke up—I think it's one of the strongest things I've ever written—but something about that tone in his voice has me second-guessing myself all of a sudden. "Why, are you not into it?"

"No, no, I think it's great," Bex says quickly, holding his hands up. "It's really smart, and thoughtful, and edgy— and obviously the writing is top-notch. I guess I just wanted to make sure you'd thought through all the angles before we published it, that's all."

I frown. "What's there to think about?"

"Well, I don't know," Bex says, tilting his head to the side. "You're taking some pretty bold positions, don't you think?"

"I guess," I say slowly. "I mean, I didn't think they were *that* bold."

"Look, Marin, don't get me wrong." Bex smiles. "It's a stellar piece. This school is just full of a bunch of dopes, that's all. As your adviser, I want to make sure you're prepared for whatever blowback might come your way."

"You think I'm going to get blowback?" I ask, surprised. The idea hadn't actually occurred to me, and all at once I wonder if that makes me completely naive. "From who?"

"I have no idea," Bex says immediately. "Not from me, obviously. I just don't want you to be taken off guard if people aren't crazy about what you have to say, that's all."

I nod, crossing my arms a little bit tighter until it almost feels like I'm hugging myself. I'm getting the distinct impression he thinks I should pull the piece altogether, and part of me wants to agree with him—after all, the last thing I want is for people around school to think I'm some kind of militant feminist.

The other part of me can't help but wonder if somehow this is related to what happened in his apartment.

"Isn't that the point of being the editor of the paper?" I ask finally, forcing myself to relax my posture, to stand up straight and push my shoulders back like someone who knows her own mind and isn't afraid to speak it. "Saying stuff that makes other people uncomfortable sometimes?"

Bex looks at me for a long moment, an inscrutable expression on his face. "Fair enough," he says, as the warning bell rings for homeroom. "We'll put it in the next issue."

The seed of doubt Bex planted in my head spends all morning growing roots and leaves and flowers; by the time third period rolls around, it's practically a national park. I'm hoping for a pep talk from Chloe before the bell rings, but when she scurries into Bex's classroom her painted eyebrows are knitted tightly together.

"Okay," she says, making a beeline down the aisle and perching on the edge of my desk, blowing a tendril of yellow hair out of her eyes and dropping her electric blue leather tote bag on the linoleum with a quiet thump. "Can we talk about your editorial for a sec?"

My heart sinks. "You don't like it either?" I ask.

"No, it's not that, I just—" Chloe frowns. "Wait, who else doesn't like it?"

I shrug, glancing over my shoulder up at the front of the room and lowering my voice. "Bex was weird about it this morning. I don't know."

"He was probably just looking out for you."

"Why do I need looking out for though? Like, what

about this piece is so bad that—"

"It's not bad!" Chloe interrupts. "It's just . . . a little . . . shrill."

My mouth drops open, stung. "What's shrill?"

"I mean, your *voice* is shrill right now, for one thing," Chloe teases gently, laughing a little. "Easy, tiger. I don't know. It just kind of sounds like you hate all boys, first of all. Or like you think you're experiencing some great oppression because you have to shave your legs. Or like you're about to turn into one of those girls who *doesn't* shave her legs in the first place."

"Of course I'm still going to shave my legs!" I protest. "That's not what I'm—"

"Look," she tells me, "I'm not saying we should pull it. And I'm not even giving you a hard time for going rogue on me, even though I thought we were supposed to be coeditors of this whole thing. I just think you should be ready for blowback, that's all."

"*Blowback?*" My eyes narrow, suddenly suspicious. That's the same word Bex used. "Did you talk to Bex about this?"

"What?" Chloe shakes her head. "No!"

For some reason I don't entirely believe her, though it's possible I'm just being paranoid. I don't totally trust my own judgment today. Make that lately.

"Okay," I say slowly. "So we'll run it?"

"We'll run it," she promises with a smile. She bumps my shoulder with hers before she sits down.

My editorial runs on the front page of the *Beacon* the following Monday, right next to the results of last week's swim meet and this week's lunch menu.

I find Jacob in the cafeteria before first period, where he's eating an egg sandwich and scrolling through Snapchat on his phone. "Hey," I call, relieved by the sight of him. I was up half the night wondering if I was making a huge mistake—opening myself up to all kinds of unnecessary drama, upsetting the status quo—but that's ridiculous, isn't it? After all, it's just an editorial. And really, is any of it even that controversial? I mean, the rules for being a girl are ridiculous. Anyone can see that.

Jacob doesn't smile back. "Hey," he says, and that's when I notice the paper spread out in front of him like a placemat.

"Don't tell me," I say, sitting cautiously down in the chair beside him. "You're not a fan."

Jacob shrugs. "It's not that I'm not a fan," he says. "It just . . . didn't make me feel very good, that's all."

"It didn't?" I ask, momentarily confused. "Why not? I mean, it's not about you."

"Maybe not," Jacob counters, "but everybody's going to think it is. Like, is this really what you think all guys are like?"

"The piece isn't even *about* guys though," I protest. "It's about the expectations on girls, that's all."

"I guess," Jacob says, sounding wholly unconvinced.

"You know, you could try to say something nice about it," I snap, suddenly irritated. "Since I'm ostensibly your girlfriend and all."

"Ostensibly my girlfriend?" Jacob's eyes narrow. "What does *that* mean?"

I glance around the cafeteria, uneasy; it's pretty empty at this hour, but we're hardly alone. I can see a pair of freshmen a few tables over pretending not to listen. "It means I would love if you could try to be a little bit more supportive, that's all," I say, lowering my voice to a murmur. "I'm sorry. I'm just not a hundred percent sure about how people are going to react to it, so—"

"So then why did you publish it in the first place?" he interrupts. "And also, like, you obviously don't care what I think either way, since you didn't even give me a heads-up—I had to hear about it from freakin' Joey, which—"

"I don't need your permission to write an editorial."

"That's not what I'm saying!" Jacob shakes his head. "Do you hear me saying that right now?" He sighs.

"Come on," he says, reaching for my hand and squeezing. "I'm sorry you're stressed out about it. If it makes you feel better, it's not like people are exactly clamoring to read the *Beacon* the second it comes out."

"Seriously?" I ask, pulling away. "Probably nobody even read it? *That's* the best you can do?"

Jacob's shoulders stiffen. "What's your *problem* this morning, huh?" he asks, sounding honestly baffled. "Are you on the rag or what?"

I blink at him for a moment. "Okay," I blurt, shoving my chair back with a loud, grating screech. Suddenly I don't care who's paying attention. "You know what? I don't think this is working."

"Wait a second." Jacob's eyes widen. "What's not working?"

"This." I gesture between us. "You and me, all of it. I think . . . maybe I just need some space. From you. Like, permanently."

I'm actually shocked to hear the words come out of my mouth, and from the look on Jacob's face, I can see he is too. Ten minutes ago, breaking up with him wasn't even on my radar. But suddenly it seems like the only logical choice.

"What the hell, Marin?" Jacob stands up too, so we're eye to eye, his chair clattering. "Where the hell is this coming from? Like, okay, I'm sorry I said that thing about you having your period. That was fucked. But it's nothing to break up over."

"Isn't it?" I ask, although now that I'm actually thinking about it, it feels like so much more than that one stupid comment. It's the list his lacrosse buddies made last year ranking freshman girls in order of hotness. It's how he laughed at Deanna in the cafeteria. It's his smirk when we talk about the dress code, and the way he always assumes I want Froyo and not ice cream. It's a million little things that I told myself didn't matter, except for all of a sudden they completely do.

"I don't know, dude."

"Fine," Jacob says, throwing his hands up. He's pissed now, his mouth gone thin and his cheeks an angry pink. "We're done, then. You know, it's probably better we break up anyway, if this is what you're going to be like now."

"Oh?" I raise my eyebrows. "And what exactly am I like?"

"Like this," he says, waving at me vaguely. "You write some weird article and start acting like a total psycho and . . .

what? Turn into some crazy feminist?"

I laugh out loud at that, a mean hollow bark. "Some crazy— You know what, Jacob? Maybe that's exactly what I'm turning into. And maybe you can go screw yourself."

For a moment Jacob just stares at me, his mouth opening and closing. I've never said anything like that before—to him, or to anyone. I'm waiting for the surge of horror, but instead I just feel kind of powerful. Maybe I should tell people to screw themselves more often.

"Okay then," he finally says, crumpling his sandwich wrapper up into a ball and chucking it into the bin at the front of the cafeteria. "See you never."

"See you never," I echo, slinging my backpack over my shoulder and heading to my first-period class.

Jacob's reaction to my editorial is a pretty good litmus test for the rest of the morning, all told. Dean Shepherd makes a big show of cowering like he thinks I'm going to hit him. Hallie Weisbuck makes a Hillary Clinton joke.

"Maybe it's a good thing," Chloe says consolingly at the beginning of Bex's class. "Honestly, this is the most people have talked about the *Beacon* since we started editing it."

"Headlines don't sell papes, Marin's crazy editorials sell papes?" I ask, riffing on *Newsies*, which we used to watch all the time back in middle school. Then I frown. "Oh, also, I just broke up with Jacob."

"Wait, what?" Chloe's hands drop. *"Why?"*

"Because——" I break off. All of a sudden *His casual sexism randomly started to bother me when he said he didn't like my piece* doesn't feel like the banner cause it did this morning. "Because——"

Chloe shakes her head. "Marin, what is going *on* with you?"

"Okay," Bex calls before I can answer, leaning against his desk up at the front of the room. "You guys ready to get started?"

I slink low in my chair as he goes over this week's vocab unit, then assigns a response paper due the following week. "I've got a new reading list for you all to take a look at," he says, passing out a stack of papers. "I want you guys to pick one of the short stories on this list, then write two to three pages on one of the literary techniques the author uses."

It's an easy assignment, the kind of thing I'll be able to knock out in an hour or two, but as I scan the list of authors I find myself frowning: John Updike, Michael Chabon, John Cheever. Before I can quell the impulse, my hand is up in the air.

"Yep," Bex says, nodding in my direction. "Uh, Marin."

"I'm sorry, I just—" I look around a little nervously. Dean Shepherd already has a smirk on his face. "Shouldn't there be some female authors on this list? Or authors who aren't white?"

Bex looks surprised for a moment; he glances down at the list, like possibly he hadn't noticed the omission. He tsks quietly, then looks back up at me. "Ooookay then, Marin," he says brightly. "Not into the list, huh? What do you think I should add?"

"Oh—um." I hesitate, my mind going completely, terrifyingly blank. In this moment I honestly couldn't name a single short story if my life depended on it, let alone one written by somebody other than a dead white guy. "I guess I hadn't really thought it through that far," I admit finally.

"Well," Bex says in that same cheerful voice—slightly plastic, I think now, more sarcasm than actual friendliness. It's the first time all year he's seemed anything less than 100 percent chill about an assignment—although I guess it's also the first time I've complained. "Make sure you let us know if you come up with anything, yeah?"

The class kind of chuckles, and I nod miserably, feeling my whole body prickle with embarrassment. Chloe shoots me an incredulous look. God, why couldn't I just have kept my mouth shut? It's not like I wasn't drawing enough attention to myself already.

Bex is turning back to the whiteboard when there's a knock on the open door. I glance over, and there's Ms. Klein in the doorway in her navy-blue shirtdress and her big round glasses, her dark hair in a tidy bun on top of her head.

"Mr. Beckett," she says, gaze flicking from him to me and back again in a way that makes me wonder if she heard the whole exchange. "I've got your attendance forms from Ms. Lynch. I told her I'd drop them off."

"Oh!" Bex nods, shooting her a megawatt smile. "Thank you."

By the time he gets back to his desk he seems to have forgotten about me, thank God. Still, I spend the rest of the period slouched in my seat, aching to disappear. Chloe makes a beeline for me once the bell rings for the end of the period, grabbing my arm and steering me out into the hallway.

"Okay, did you seriously need to add picking a fight with Bex in front of the whole class to the list of dramatic things you did today?" she asks, joking, but also not really. "Do you have raging PMS or what?"

"Oh, come on." I don't tell her I dumped Jacob for

basically saying that exact thing to me not three hours ago. "I wasn't picking a fight," I defend myself instead. "It just felt like—"

"Marin!"

I flinch. I cannot take one more person giving me shit today. But when I turn around it's Ms. Klein, holding her water bottle in one hand and a slim white paperback in the other. "Can I talk to you for a minute?"

"Um." I look from her to Chloe and back again. "Sure," I say, and follow Ms. Klein down the hall.

"I overheard your conversation with Mr. Beckett," she tells me, and I grimace.

"I don't know that I'd call that a conversation," I admit. "I totally froze."

Ms. Klein smiles. "It happens," she says. "But it was a good impulse on your part—an all-white, all-male reading list is ridiculous. Next time you'll have to be better prepared, that's all. Here"—she holds out the book for my inspection—"this might be a good place to start."

I look down at the title: *Bad Feminist*, by Roxane Gay.

"You know," she says, looking at me thoughtfully, "if you're not happy with the way things are around here, you ought to do something about it."

She heads down the hallway before I can ask her what

she means exactly, then turns back to face me. "By the way," she calls, "I really liked your article."

I read *Bad Feminist* in the library at lunchtime and in between classes and tucked into my bed late at night, and two mornings later I go to see Ms. Klein before the first-period bell rings. She's sitting in the bio lab going over lesson plans, classical music playing softly on her phone beside her. Her shirtdress is a deep hunter green.

"Hi, Marin," she says, smiling. "How'd it go with the book?"

"I think I have an idea," I tell her, instead of answering. "But I need your help."

TWELVE

"I'm just warning you now, I don't think anyone's going to come," I tell Ms. Klein two weeks later, after Thanksgiving break, perching nervously on the edge of a lab bench after the eighth-period bell. When I first had the idea for a feminist book club, the night after she gave me the Roxane Gay book, it seemed almost brilliant—what a great *fuck you* to Mr. DioGuardi's ridiculous dress code and Bex's sexist reading list, right? What a great *fuck you* to everything that's been going on. I made fliers and agonized over our first book before finally deciding on *The Handmaid's Tale* because that was what the library had the most copies of; I filed new-student-organization paperwork with Ms. Lynch in the admin suite.

Now that it's the day of our first meeting though, I just feel like the host of a party nobody wants to come to: even Chloe begged off in favor of an extra shift at the restaurant, which probably shouldn't have surprised me at this point but still sort of sucked. The fact that I couldn't convince my own best friend that a feminist book club was a good idea doesn't bode super well for its success.

Ms. Klein shrugs. "So then no one comes," she says. "You and I can talk about the book ourselves." She nods at the Dunkin' Donuts box on the desk beside her. "And eat twenty-five Munchkins apiece."

I laugh, which calms me down a little; I'm about to ask her if she's read anything else by Margaret Atwood when a couple of nervous-looking freshmen I vaguely recognize as members of the jazz band sidle into the classroom. My heart leaps when I realize they're both holding copies of the book.

"Hey," the taller one says, a white girl with her blond hair in two Princess Leia buns, looking around with no small amount of trepidation. "Um, is this the book club?"

"Sure is," Ms. Klein says. "Have a seat."

It's a little bit awkward, but to my surprise a handful of other people trickle in one by one: this kid Dave, an AV dude with carroty hair and a pale face full of freckles, and Lydia Jones, who's black and works on the lit mag. Elisa Hernandez, the five-foot-tall captain of the girls' volleyball team, shows up with a couple of her teammates.

"You guys have a big game coming up, right?" Ms. Klein asks, and Elisa beams.

"We were state champs last year," she explains with a nod. "We're defending our title."

"Seriously?" I ask, surprised. I don't exactly have my ear to the ground around school lately, but I've heard exactly nothing about this. I think of how everybody—me included—always shows up to cheer for our sucky football team, even though they won like twice all of last season. "How come they're not doing a pep rally for you guys?"

"Are you kidding?" Elisa asks, as her teammates giggle. "We can barely even get a bus for away games most of the time."

I frown. "That's so obnoxious." It's like now that I'm looking for inequality I'm seeing it everywhere, categorizing a thousand great and small unfairnesses everywhere I go. Why didn't I really see this before?

"Sounds like a great topic for your next op-ed, Marin," Ms. Klein says pointedly, popping a Munchkin into her mouth.

Which—huh. I look over at Elisa, raising my eyebrows.

"You want to do an interview?" I ask, and Elisa grins.

Eventually Ms. Klein steers us back around to *The Handmaid's Tale*. I've never been in a book club before, and I printed a list of discussion questions off the internet in case there were any horrifying lulls in the conversation, but it turns out we don't even need them: Lydia and Elisa are big talkers, and Dave is quietly hilarious, with a sense of humor so darkly dry it takes me a full beat to realize when he's joking. We're talking about the similarities between the Republic of Gilead and modern-day America when somebody knocks on the open door. I look up, and there's Gray Kendall in his Bridgewater Lax hoodie, backpack slung over one bulky shoulder.

"Uh," he says, his dark eyes flicking around the room. "Sorry I'm late. Is this the book club meeting?"

Right away I sit up a little straighter. "Why?"

"Marin," Ms. Klein chides mildly. "You're looking at it, Gray."

"Cool," Gray says. He looks at me a little strangely, then holds up a book—a battered paperback copy of *The Handmaid's Tale*, a bright orange USED SAVES sticker peeling off the spine. "Can I, uh—?"

"You did not read that book," I blurt before I can stop

myself. I know I'm being hugely rude, but he's obviously got some kind of ulterior motive. For one insane second I wonder if Jacob sent him to mess with me.

"Um." Gray huffs a laugh, good-natured but slightly disbelieving. "Yeah, I did."

My eyes narrow. "The whole thing?"

"Yeah."

I look at him skeptically, trying to figure out what on earth his game is. A random lax bro showing up here like some kind of Trojan horse who's acting all interested to try and . . . what? Infiltrate my book club? That makes no sense.

Everyone else is watching silently. Dave clears his throat.

"Fine," I say eventually. "You can stay."

Gray smiles then, saluting me with his tattered paperback and making his way to an empty seat across the circle. Ms. Klein asks a question about Offred and the Commander, and the discussion is pretty animated from there. I'm expecting Gray to try to dominate the conversation, but to my surprise he mostly keeps his mouth shut; when I glance over in his direction he's leaning slightly forward in his seat, listening to Elisa with a furrowed brow. He's *so* quiet, in fact, that as we're about to wrap up, Ms. Klein nods in his direction.

"You've been keeping to yourself over there, Gray," she says pleasantly. "Anything you took from the book that we haven't covered?"

"Um." Gray clears his throat. "I mean, I'll be honest, I thought it was terrifying. My heart was pounding the whole entire time. I almost peed my pants when that girl's plane to Canada got stopped on the runway."

I frown. That definitely didn't happen in the book, unless I somehow missed it. "Which girl?" I ask; Lydia and Elisa look at him curiously.

"The main one," he explains, for once in his life looking vaguely uncomfortable at the prospect of this much female attention at once. "You know, the one who was on *Mad Men*."

And there it is. "Uh-huh," I say, satisfied. "That's what I thought."

"All right," Ms. Klein says, barely hiding a smile. "We should break up for today anyway, but I'll meet you all back here next week." We're going to read mostly short stories and essays, we decided, for the sake of being able to meet more frequently. "Any of you who want to take leftover Munchkins home, feel free."

I pocket a couple of glazed and head out to the parking lot, where I'm surprised to catch Gray pacing back and forth in front of the building, stopping every few feet to frown down at what looks like his watch.

"You okay over there?" I call out.

Gray nods sheepishly. "Step counter," he calls by way of explanation, waggling his wrist in my direction. "But it's not working."

I laugh, I can't help it. "Seriously?" I don't know what it is about this guy that makes me want to heckle him.

"What's wrong with a step counter?"

I shake my head, walking closer. "I mean, nothing, if you're my mom."

"Is your mom extremely physically fit?" Gray fires back.

"If Zumba counts, absolutely she is." I nod at his wrist. "What's your goal?"

"Twenty thousand."

I raise my eyebrows and shrug my peacoat around my shoulders. "Every day?"

He shrugs. "It's not that much, really."

"You don't have to have false modesty about your step count," I say with a smile. "I'm not that impressed."

"Clearly," Gray says, grinning back. I can't tell if he's flirting with me or not. Even if he is, I know it doesn't mean anything. Gray is notorious for flirting with everyone.

"So what were you really doing in there, huh?" I can't resist asking, nodding my head back toward the building. "With the book club, I mean."

Gray makes a face. "College apps," he admits. "I need to bulk up extracurriculars." He tilts his head to the side. "I thought it was ballsy how you fought with Mr. Beckett though. So I came to support. Or like——" He frowns. "I guess *ballsy* isn't the right word, huh?"

I shake my head. "*Ballsy* is fine."

"*Brave* is what I meant."

I smile again, more slowly, and this time nothing about it is a tease. "I'm sorry I gave you a hard time in there," I tell him.

"It's cool," Gray says. "I get it." The strangest part is how it seems like maybe he does. I think of his serious expression when Jacob made that stupid joke at Emily's party, the way he always sort of seems to keep his distance from the rest of the lacrosse guys. Just for a moment, I wonder if possibly there's more to Gray Kendall than I thought.

My phone rings inside my backpack—the kicky little trill that means it's my mom—but when I go for it the busted zipper on the bottom pouch catches again. I swear quietly, yanking with absolutely no success whatsoever.

"It's just stuck," I explain, a little awkwardly. "I probably just need a new one."

Gray shakes his head. "You got ChapStick? Actually, you know what, never mind. I do." He digs a tube of it out of his pack pocket and uncaps it with his teeth, rubbing the stick along the zipper until it slides open without a problem. "There," he says, dimple flashing as he hands it back over. "Good as new, right?"

"Yeah," I say, smiling back in spite of myself. "Good as new."

THIRTEEN

"Hey there, Marin," Chloe's dad says, grinning at me from behind the bar when I come into Niko's that night. "I read your article. Very good."

I grin back, rolling my eyes a little. "Thanks."

"I'm serious," he says cheerfully.

I've always liked Steve, with his thick eyebrows and beer belly and incessantly corny dad jokes.

"You go, girl."

"Oh my god," Chloe says, brushing by behind me and heading for the kitchen. "Dad, can you stay out of feminist politics for today?"

Steve frowns, rubbing a hand over his bushy beard as he watches her go. I just shrug.

I catch up with her back by the wait station, where she's tying on her apron.

"Hey," I offer a sheepish smile. "I hardly saw you today. Everything okay?"

"I'm fine," Chloe says immediately, offering me a quick smile. "It's just been super busy."

I feel my lips twist; I've never *not* spent so much time with Chloe as I have this past week. "You sure?"

"Totally," she says. "How was your book club?"

"Good!" I say with a smile, surprised to find that I mean it, and launch into a detailed description of our meeting. I'm telling her about our plan to make *Nolite te bastardes carborundorum* T-shirts for next week's dress-down day before I realize she isn't listening at all.

"You should think about joining," I finish weakly. Then, "Chlo, what's *wrong?*"

Chloe sighs. "Look," she says, "this is probably going to sound bitchy, and I honestly don't mean for it to, but like. You're just so *different* lately. Like, where's Marin? My fun, cool best friend Marin?"

She holds her hands up, glancing over her shoulder toward the dining room. "I know you've had some . . .

stuff . . . ," she says meaningfully. "But I thought you were going to put all that behind you. And instead you're just like . . . rolling around in it, I don't know."

I blink. "Rolling around in what, exactly?"

"Don't get mad," Chloe says. "I just—"

"Ladies!" Steve calls, deep voice booming from behind the bar. "Tables, please."

We don't talk for the rest of the night, orbiting around each other like two competing moons. Yes, I've had some *stuff*, I think to myself, a little bitterly. And I have put it behind me, obviously. I didn't tell anyone. I'm still doing everything I was doing before. But I'm also thinking about things a little differently. Is there something wrong with that?

By nine thirty, I've had enough. This is ridiculous, I decide finally. *Where's Marin? I'm right* here. I drop the check for the last of my tables, two middle-aged guys I'm pretty sure were celebrating their anniversary. It's *me*. It's *Chloe*. I'll see if she wants to get a late-night Starbucks on the ride home. We'll listen to the new Sia album on Spotify and talk it out.

When I stow my apron and head out into the parking lot though, I look around for a long moment before I frown. Chloe has driven me home from every shift since she got her license last summer, but I don't see her SUV—a tan Jeep with a cartoon sloth bumper sticker affixed to the back window—anywhere.

I yank my phone out of my backpack. *Did you leave?* I text.

Her reply comes thirty seconds later. *ACK I'M SO SORRY! Asked my dad to tell you, but he must have spaced. Kyra's having a boy crisis so I said I'd go see her. Can you find a ride???*

If I think too much about the likelihood that Chloe has really ditched me for her dorky cousin Kyra, I might lose it, so instead I sit down on a bench outside the restaurant and consider my options for getting home: it's too far to walk. My parents are at a scholarship fund-raiser Grace's chess teacher throws every year all the way in Burlington. And I sure as shit can't call Jacob. I scroll through my phone, trying to figure out which of my friends I haven't alienated recently who might also have access to a car. Nothing like standing alone in the parking lot of a strip mall outside a Greek restaurant at ten on a Friday night to put your life choices in glaring perspective.

I'm about to go back inside and throw myself on Steve's mercy when a thought occurs to me. I bite my lip, swiping through my contacts until I find Gray's name. He put his number in there himself after the book club meeting today, then texted himself so he'd have mine: "In case I need help with the big words," he explained, handing my phone back to me with a flourish.

Hey, I text now, hitting send before I can talk myself out of it. *Are you busy?*

He shows up fifteen minutes later, pulling to the curb outside the restaurant in a ten-year-old Toyota with a bobblehead dog affixed to the dashboard. "Somebody call an Uber?" he asks as I climb in.

"Hey," I say with a grateful grin. "Thank you. You're totally saving me right now."

"No problem." His car smells like cinnamon Altoids and a little bit like a gym bag; his phone is upside down in the cupholder, Kendrick Lamar echoing quietly from the tinny speaker. "No Bluetooth," he explains, a little sheepish.

"I'm going to have to dock you a star," I tease, nudging aside a half-dozen empty Pepsi bottles and setting my backpack on the floor between my feet. "Seriously, though, I mean it. Thanks. I didn't think you'd be around."

"Because I'm so popular?"

I make a face. "I mean, you're more popular than me right now, that's for sure."

Gray doesn't comment. "I was out with some friends," he admits, glancing over his shoulder before pulling out onto the main road, "but I was tired of them anyway."

"You were, huh?"

"Yeah," he says easily. "I'll be honest with you, Marin. I've been thinking I need a change."

He's full of shit, clearly, but I smile anyway. I lean my head against the back of the seat rest. "You and me both."

"So, um," he says. "Where to?"

"Oh, crap!" I laugh and give him my address. "You can just drop me at the corner of Oak if you don't want to deal with the roundabout. I can walk the rest of the way."

"Now what kind of Uber driver would I be if I did that?" Gray asks with a grin. Then: "Hey, are you hungry?"

I literally just ate half a tray of spanakopita, but . . . "Are *you*?"

"I mean, I'm seventeen," he says, grinning crookedly. "I'm literally always hungry."

We stop at the Executive Diner on Route 4, following a stern-looking waitress to a booth by the window. I order a peanut butter milk shake while Gray gets a cheeseburger with onion rings and a side of chocolate chip pancakes. "I've never actually been in here at night before," he says, looking around at the chipped Formica tables, the few schleppy middle-aged dudes posted up at the bar.

"Oh no?" I ask, wrinkling my nose at him over my milk shake. "Too busy wining and dining the ladies of Bridgewater Prep?"

"Or writing feminist op-eds," he counters with a smile.

"Or getting kicked out of fancy schools for being a degenerate?"

I'm teasing, but Gray flinches a little. "Is that what I did?" he asks, raising his dark eyebrows across the table.

"Isn't it?" I ask. "I mean, I heard . . ." I trail off. "Shit. I'm sorry. I'm an asshole."

"Nah, you're fine." Gray smiles, dunking one of his onion rings in a ketchup/mayo/hot sauce concoction of his own making. "I don't know how that rumor got started. I mean, I do, I like to throw parties, but that's not what I got expelled for."

"So what happened, then?" I ask, stirring my milk shake with a long metal spoon instead of looking at him. "I mean, you don't have to tell me, obviously."

"No, it's cool." He shrugs. "I was too dumb."

My head snaps up. "You're not dumb," I say immediately.

Gray waves a hand. "I mean, sure, not *dumb*, but . . . I've got, like, ADD and stuff, and was not meeting Hartley's, uh, rigorous academic standards."

I frown. "Don't they have to accommodate you for that?" I ask. "It's a disability, no?"

"I mean, sure," Gray says. "But you also have to like . . . do your work every once in a while."

"Ah," I say, feeling my face relax into a smile. "Right. I can see how that would be part of the bargain."

"Yeah. Anyway," Gray continues, "people are going to think what they want to think about you, right? So I just kind of . . . let them think it. It's a better story, in any case."

"But don't you ever want to set the record straight?" I dip my fork in his ketchupy sauce, tasting cautiously. Not bad.

Gray shrugs. "Sure, sometimes," he says, "if it's somebody whose opinion I give a shit about. But mostly I feel like: it's only a few more months, right? What do I care?"

"I guess," I say slowly. "Where are you headed next year, do you know?"

Gray groans, pretending to upend his plate of pancakes and slither onto the floor underneath the booth—only then he almost *does* knock over his Pepsi, grabbing the big plastic cup at the last second. His reflexes are impressive, I've got to give him that much.

"Uh-oh," I say with a laugh. "Sorry. Touchy subject?"

Gray sighs, scrubbing a hand over his face. "Both my moms are lawyers, right? Or actually, it's worse—one of them is a lawyer, and the other one is a law *professor.* And both of them went to St. Lawrence, and both of them want me to go there and play lacrosse, because they donate a ton of money there every year, so it's like the one place I'm guaranteed to get in even though I'm an idiot."

"Stop saying that," I tell him, kicking him under the table before I quite know I'm going to do it. "You're not an idiot. What do *you* want to do?"

"Paint," Gray deadpans, his face heartbreakingly serious for a moment before it busts wide open into a goofy grin. "No, I'm kidding. I kind of don't want to go at all, honestly. I had to volunteer at this after-school program in Fall River for community service last year—which, yeah, I'm not saying that everything you heard about my partying was a lie."

"Laundry detergent?" I ask, raising my eyebrows.

"I didn't tell anyone to eat laundry detergent!" Gray says, sounding outraged. "Like, Jesus, I'm the one with the fucking learning disability and even I know enough not to eat soap."

I snort. "Fair enough."

"Anyway, I had to go there three times a week and play games with these little kids, and at first it was a total drag, but I actually really liked it, so I still go, even though I did all my hours. And they like me too, I guess, because they offered me a full-time gig after graduation if I want it."

"That's awesome," I say—picturing it before I can

stop myself, trying not to find it charming and failing completely. "But your parents—your moms, I mean—aren't on board?"

Gray grimaces. "Oh, no way. Not go to college? As far as they're concerned I might as well sell my body for drug money. Or like, go work for the US government."

Gray finishes his burger-and-pancake feast, plus a slice of questionable cheesecake from the spinning case near the cashier; his shoulder bumps mine as we head outside into the raw, chilly night.

"Can I ask you a rude question?" I say as we cross the parking lot. "If your grades are really that bad, what are you doing in AP English?"

Gray snorts. "It was the only language arts requirement that would fit in my schedule," he explains, clicking the button to unlock the doors to the Toyota. "They made an exception so I could play lacrosse. Which," he says, obviously reading the expression on my face in the neon light coming off the diner sign, "I recognize is probably the same special treatment that makes it so the girls' volleyball team doesn't get a bus."

"Wait—" I start, remembering Gray wasn't even there when we started talking about that.

"I was standing outside the door before I came in," he

explains. "I was nervous."

I smile at that, sliding back into the passenger seat. "It's a fucked-up system, that's all. And for what it's worth, I'm really glad you're in that class with me. And I'm glad you came to book club."

"Yeah," he says. "I'm glad I am too."

We ride to my house mostly in silence, just the sound of Gray's tinny iPhone speaker and the slightly labored hum of the Toyota's engine.

"Thanks again," I tell him when we pull up in front of my house. "You really bailed me out."

"Yeah, no problem," he says. "I'll see you Monday."

"See you Monday," I echo, reaching down for my backpack. I've got my hand on the car door when he touches my arm.

"Hey, Marin, by the way?" Gray clears his throat, like maybe he's a tiny bit nervous again. "I, um. Really liked your article."

I laugh out loud, surprised and weirdly delighted, but then it's like the laugh jangles something loose in me, and for a moment I think I might be about to burst into tears.

Instead, I take a deep breath and smile at him in the green glow of the dashboard.

"Thanks."

FOURTEEN

Saturday night finds me sitting at my desk in my pajamas, trying to keep my eyes from glazing over as I scroll boringly through an ancient SparkNotes guide to the symbolism in "The Swimmer." Chloe ended up spending the weekend with Kyra, so instead of hitting Starbucks or driving around singing along to her latest Spotify masterpiece like we usually would, I'm listening to Sam Smith, picking at my short-story paper for Bex's class, and—okay, I can admit it—thinking about Gray. I'm not looking for a new boyfriend, obviously. But still. I liked talking to him. I liked the feeling that he actually cared about what I had to say.

I'm making zero progress on this paper, meanwhile. Part of me just wants to say screw Bex and go rogue and write it on the Hunger Games essay from *Bad Feminist*, but what good would that do? I'd just be hurting myself in the end.

Grace knocks on my open door. "Will you do that thing with the flat iron?" she asks, holding it up and rotating it in a circle to demonstrate.

"Sure," I say, feeling my eyebrows flick before I can quell the impulse. She's dressed in skinny jeans and a crop top I'm not entirely sure my mom is going to let her wear out of the house, plus a pair of wedge booties that are definitely mine. "Where are your glasses?" I ask, ignoring the petty theft for now in favor of getting up and rolling the desk chair in front of the full-length mirror on the back of my closet door.

Grace shrugs, a quick jerk of her shoulders. "I don't need them."

That is . . . some magical thinking if ever I've heard it. "Gracie," I say, struggling not to laugh, "you're basically straight-up blind without your glasses. You're going to be walking into walls like Mr. Magoo."

Grace flops down into the chair, sighing loudly in the direction of the hallway. "Well if Mom would just let me get contacts, that wouldn't matter."

"Why *does* it matter, huh?" I ask, frowning a little as I reach down to plug the flat iron into the wall. "Where are you even going?"

"Just to the movies with some people in my class."

"Some people . . . ," I echo, scooping my own hair out of my face and sensing there's more to the story here. "Any person in particular?"

Gracie tilts her head back, her long brown hair reaching almost to the carpet. "I mean, there's a boy," she admits grudgingly. "But it's not a big deal."

"Oh yeah?" I gather up her hair in both hands, raking through the tangles and betting on the fact that she'll say more if and only if I act like I'm not curious. "Grab me that claw clip, will you?"

Sure enough: "His name is Louis," she continues, handing it over; I divide her hair into sections as I wait for the iron to heat up. "And he's so cute. And when we talk in Spanish I think he likes me—like, he's always laughing at my jokes and stuff—but he's popular." She screws her face up in the mirror, or maybe she's just squinting to try to see herself. "And just, with the glasses, and the chess—"

"You *love* chess!" I blurt, unable to help it. "And you're fucking amazing at it, so—"

119

"That's not the point!" Grace interrupts. "The other girls in my class . . ." She trails off. "They have boobs, and one of them has eyelash extensions. And I basically still look like a little kid."

You are *a little kid*, I think immediately, but at least I know better than to say it out loud. I gaze at Gracie in the mirror, her clear skin and straight eyebrows, the scar on the edge of her mouth from the time she took a header off her skateboard when she was seven. I want to tell her that Opal Cosare was the first person to get boobs in my class and the boys made her life a living hell over it. I want to tell her that getting older isn't everything it's cracked up to be. But I don't want to scare her off.

I'm quiet for a moment, clamping her hair in the flat iron and pulling gently. Chloe taught me this trick, I think with a tiny pang behind my rib cage, patiently doing it for me until I figured it out for myself.

"Anybody who doesn't think you're adorable in your glasses isn't worth it anyway," I say finally, flicking my wrist to make a perfect fashion-blogger wave.

"You have to say that," Gracie retorts, rolling her eyes. "It's like, in the big-sister constitution. Next thing you'll be telling me is I'm perfect just the way I am."

"I mean, you *are* perfect the way you are," I tell her.

"But it's not like I didn't go through this exact thing in eighth grade. Remember when I begged Mom to let me get a belly button ring before that pool party at Tamar Harris's house?"

"Oh my god, I forgot about that," Grace says, grinning goofily. "You kept threatening to do it yourself with a sewing needle."

"I don't even think there *are* any sewing needles in our house," I say with a laugh. "Like, when was the last time you saw Mom sew something? But I just thought that belly button ring was the key to my glamorous teenage life or something, I don't even know." I remember the run-up to that party with a kind of visceral embarrassment—the girl who searched high and low for the perfect two-piece and attempted to contour a six-pack onto her stomach with makeup, wanting to prove how chill and fun and sexy she was on the eve of her middle school graduation—and at the same time I wish I could go back and protect her.

"Anyway," I say now, tilting Grace's head to the side to get to the section of hair behind her ear, "if you honestly don't want to be wearing glasses anymore because you personally like how you look better without them, I'll help you pitch it to Mom for this summer. But if you're just doing it to try to impress Louis—or anybody else—I can promise you that tripping down a flight of stairs at the Alewife multiplex is not going to get you the kind of attention you're after."

"I *guess*," Grace grumbles, visibly unconvinced.

Then she turns her face to look at me. "I thought your article was really good, PS," she says suddenly. "I don't know if I told you that or not. "

"Really?" I peer at her in the mirror, surprised. "How did you even read it?"

"My friend McKenna had a copy," she explains. "Her sister goes to your school."

"Oh." I nod. "Cool. Thanks, Gracie." I think about that for a moment, busying myself with the flat iron to hide my smile. Realistically, I know that my feminist book club and my editorials in the paper probably aren't going to make a whole lot of difference to the world at large. But if they made some kind of difference to my sister, that would be something.

"Promise me you'll wear your glasses tonight, okay?" I ask her, pulling the barrette out of her hair and clamping it onto the pocket of my hoodie for safekeeping. "If only so that I don't have to visit you in the ER instead of finishing this paper."

Gracie hums noncommittally, her fuzzy gaze flicking to the open laptop sitting on my desk. She doesn't say anything, but for a moment I can see her thinking it, weighing the cost of everything I've been up to lately: no boyfriend. No plans on a Saturday night. Big-sister constitution or not, I'm half expecting her to tell me to mind my own business.

"Fine," she finally declares. "I'll wear them."

This time I don't bother to hide my smile. "Good," I tell her, satisfied. "Now stop moving around so I can finish your hair."

FIFTEEN

I drop my paper on "The Swimmer" on Bex's desk on Monday, then spend the rest of class slouching silently in my seat while everyone else discusses the different point-of-view characters in *As I Lay Dying*, which we were supposed to finish over the weekend. I used to look forward to AP English all morning, but the last few weeks it's like I spend the entire period holding my breath and hoping to disappear.

Today I feel like maybe I actually have turned invisible, until nearly the very end of the period, when Bex catches my eye across the room.

"Marin," he says, "you've been quiet today. Any thoughts

you'd like to share on our old friend Billy Faulkner?"

"Um." I swallow hard, my heart skittering like a mouse along a baseboard. I don't like this version of myself. I don't recognize her. "Nope," I say, clearing my throat a bit. "I don't think so."

"Really?" Bex raises his eyebrows in surprise that might or might not be genuine. "Nothing to add?"

I shake my head. A month ago, I would have fallen all over myself to come up with something witty and intelligent and impressive. This morning, I can't bring myself to try. "I think everybody else has pretty much covered it," I manage to say.

I'm expecting him to leave me alone after that—Bex has never been the kind of teacher who's interested in embarrassing anybody for the sake of proving a point—but instead he keeps his gaze on mine, steady. "Did you not do the reading or something?" he asks.

"What?" I ask, hearing an edge in my voice. "Of course I did."

"Okay." Bex shrugs. "Then what?"

"Then nothing," I snap, suddenly out of patience for whatever game he's trying to play. "I'm just saying, it's hard to get worked up about the literary themes in a book where one woman character dies in the first twenty pages and the other one spends the whole time getting taken advantage of by creepy men while she tries to get an abortion, that's all."

For a second the classroom is so quiet I can hear my own heartbeat. Then a chorus of laughs and *ooh*s break out. Chloe whirls around to stare at me, her eyes shocked and wide-looking; Gray lifts his chin in a wry, delighted nod.

Only Bex's face is completely impassive, and that's how I can tell I've gone too far. Sure, we've always joked around in his class, made fun of the books we're reading and the authors who wrote them, but this . . .

This wasn't that.

I'm opening my mouth to apologize, but he holds up a hand to stop me.

"See?" is all he says, and his voice is so, so even. "I knew you'd have an opinion." He nods at the door as the bell rings for the end of the period. "Class dismissed."

My interview at Brown is first thing Saturday morning. I wake up as dawn is dragging itself blue and gray over the horizon, then spend close to an hour obsessing over my outfit: if I wear a dress, does that make me seem unserious? If I *don't* wear a dress, am I saying something else? I finally decide on a pair of skinny black pants and a lacy blue button down, plus an off-white cardigan that belongs to my mom. I add a lucky bracelet that used to be my gram's, then steal my wedge booties back out of Gracie's room and head downstairs, where my parents are drinking coffee at the kitchen table.

"You look fierce," my mom says with an approving nod.

"'Though she be but little,'" my dad says, raising his mug in a salute. "That's Shakespeare, in case you want to work it into your interview. You know, show 'em how smart you are, tell 'em you got it from your old dad."

"She's not so little anymore," my mom reminds him, rolling her eyes affectionately before turning to me. "You ready to go?"

I hesitate for a moment, all the uncertainty that has been building up the last couple of weeks cresting inside me like a wave. "I mean," I say, and I'm only half kidding, "I don't actually *need* the Ivy League, right?"

"Get out of here," my dad says, pulling me close with his free hand and dropping a kiss on top of my head. "No time for cold feet."

My mom pours the rest of her coffee into a travel mug before ushering me out into the garage and turning on both seat warmers. Theoretically I could drive myself—Providence is only about forty-five minutes away—but I'm happy for the company. I lean my head back against the seat and watch the barren trees out the window, listening to the hum of the college station out of Boston she likes to listen to.

Eventually we pull off the highway and into downtown Providence, past the big mall and the river and the cute shops and restaurants nestled along Thayer Street.

"I'm going to go find a Starbucks to read in," my mom says once she finds a place to pull over near campus, leaning across the gearshift and wrapping me in a lavender-scented hug. "Text me when you're done."

She leans back and looks at me for a moment—tucking a piece of my hair back behind my ear, then smiling. "You nervous?" she asks.

"Nah," I lie.

"Mm-hmm. Just be yourself," she says—unfooled, clearly, and reaching over to hug me one more time. "If they're smart, they'll love you for it."

I can't help but smile as I shut the passenger door behind me: after all, it's exactly what I told Grace the other night, isn't it? *Just be yourself.* Never mind the fact that lately I'm not 100 percent sure who that is.

I've got a little time to kill before I meet my interviewer, so I take a lap around the bustling campus—I do find Beckett Auditorium, and my stomach turns a bit—before taking a seat on the student center steps to wait.

I spy a girl in a head scarf with a guitar case strapped to her back and a dopey-looking white guy with an absurd hipster handlebar mustache and two pretty brunettes sharing a green-tea doughnut, their gloved hands intertwined. The best part is the way none of them are gazing back at me with any particular interest, like in this place I could be whoever I want.

My interviewer is a Brown alum named Kalina who graduated a few years ago but stayed on campus to work in the admissions office; she's tall and black and willowy-looking, her dark hair in long dreads down her back. We sit in the café on campus while she asks me about my classes and my extracurriculars, what projects I'd worked on that meant the most to me.

"I read the piece you sent," she says, taking a sip of her latte. She's wearing a bright orange silk blouse and a slouchy pair of wool pants, and I immediately want to be exactly like her when I grow up.

"'The Rules for Being a Girl.' I have to tell you, I was really impressed."

I smile and duck my head, pleased but not wanting to seem too cocky—which, I think suddenly, is probably something I wouldn't worry about if I were a guy. I force myself to lift my face again, looking her square in the eye.

"Thanks," I say, and my voice hardly shakes at all. "I worked hard on it."

"I could tell." Kalina nods. "What prompted you to write something like that?"

I hesitate. *Well, my AP English teacher kissed me at his apartment* doesn't seem like a great story to lead with in a college interview—but that's not even the whole reason I wrote it, really.

"It feels like there are all these double standards for guys and girls," I explain finally, wrapping my hands around my coffee cup. "In life, I mean, but especially in high school. Once I started noticing them, it was like I couldn't stop. And it seems to me like before we can do anything—before we can, like, start to undo them—at the very least we need to point them out."

Kalina nods at that, jotting something down in her Moleskin notebook. She asks me what I see myself doing after college—journalism, I explain, though I know it's hard to make a living that way—and eventually the conversation meanders around to living in Providence and whether it's actually going to snow here later like the forecast says.

"I hope not," she says with a grimace. "I'm from Texas, and I'd never even owned a pair of snow boots before I moved here. I'm still getting used to New England winters."

"Was it a difficult adjustment?" I ask.

"I was definitely homesick at first," Kalina says, sitting back in her chair and seeming to consider it. "And honestly, this campus is pretty white. It's better now than it was when I was a student, but there's still a long way to go."

I think of the students I saw milling outside—to be honest, it seems a lot more diverse than my high school, and it occurs to me with a jolt how little I've thought about that. The same way most guys don't realize what it's really like just *being* a girl, I realize now, I definitely haven't given enough thought to what it's like just *being* black or brown, or speaking another language, or being from another place.

"I can definitely appreciate that."

Kalina nods. "So I think that's all I've got for you," she says, shutting her notebook and offering me a wide smile. "Here, let me give you my card, so you can be in touch if anything comes up. I'd wish you luck, but honestly, Marin—with your grades and extracurriculars, you shouldn't really need it."

"Really?" I can't keep the dorky excitement out of my voice. "You think so?"

"Really," she says, reaching across the table to shake my hand like a promise.

SIXTEEN

The next day I head over to Sunrise to see Gram. She's working on the *Globe* crossword puzzle when I knock on the door of her suite, tapping a ballpoint pen idly against her lipsticked mouth.

"Granola bars," I report, setting the Tupperware on the coffee table in the sitting area. "Gracie made them."

Gram raises her eyebrows. "Sounds healthy," she says ominously.

"They've got chocolate chips," I tell her, settling down beside her on the narrow love seat and breathing in her familiar grapefruit and tropical-flower smell.

"You can hardly taste the chia."

Gram smirks. "Here," she says, handing me the paper and sitting back against the throw pillows. "Help me with this. I'm useless at the pop culture clues."

I glance down at the puzzle, surprised to see it's almost all the way filled in already. "Looks like you've been doing fine without me."

Gram waves her hand. "The *Globe* puzzle is easy," she demurs, though I can tell she's a little bit pleased with herself. "They say it keeps your brain sharp, for all the good that'll do me."

"No, it will!" I say, smiling a little awkwardly. I never know exactly how to react when Gram mentions being sick. The reality is that Alzheimer's is progressive; she isn't ever going to get better, or move out of Sunrise and back into her own place. The trick, my mom always says, is to enjoy her while we have her—which, I remind myself, is exactly what I came here to do.

I open the tub of granola bars—Gram's right, they do taste a little on the healthy side—and grab the pitcher of iced tea from the fridge. We fill in the rest of the crossword while I tell her about my Brown interview.

"She basically said I was a shoo-in," I finish with a grin.

"Damn right you are," Gram says, raising her glass

in an iced tea cheers. "I'd expect nothing less from you, Marin-girl."

"What were *you* like back in college?" I ask, remembering suddenly what she told me about not having been such a good girl when she was my age. "Were you really a hell-raiser?"

"I had my moments." She glances at me over the tops of her glasses. "I got arrested in Boston once, protesting the Vietnam War."

"What?" My jaw drops. "You did *not*."

"Why is that so difficult to believe?" Gram looks openly delighted with herself now, her blue eyes bright and canny. "Oh, I swore to your grandpa I'd never tell anyone. I don't even think your mother knows."

"No, I don't think she does either." I try to imagine it— Gram with her pearl stud earrings and sensible slacks from Eileen Fisher. "You were a badass."

"Well." Gram breaks a granola bar in half. "I suppose I was. But it didn't feel like that at the time. It just felt necessary, that's all. Doing what I could to right what was wrong."

"Did you burn your bra too?" I laugh.

Gram raises her eyebrows.

I clap a hand over my mouth. "Gram!"

"Oh, it was the sixties," she says, waving her hand with

a shrug. "No one was wearing a bra to begin with."

I laugh at that. "Anything else you want to tell me about his secret life you've been hiding for the last, oh, seventeen years?"

Gram considers that for a moment. "Well, my first protests were during the civil rights movement," she tells me. "I went down to Washington for Dr. King's speech, with my church group, but you knew that."

"Grandma, I most certainly did *not* know that." I gawk at her, dumbfounded.

"Well," she says, brushing crumbs off her lap. "I suppose I always felt I could have done more—I *know* I could have done more, actually—so it didn't seem right to go around flying my own flag about it. "

I nod slowly, thinking of one of the essays in *Bad Feminist*—the one about the movie *The Help* and how it was a work of science fiction, not historical fiction. I remember watching it with my mom when I was home sick once; I'm embarrassed to admit I thought it was really inspiring, not realizing there was this whole racist narrative about a white lady swooping in to heroically combat inequality, when in reality of course the black women had been fighting their own battles for years and years. The more I read and learn lately, the more work I know I have to do.

"So what happened?" I ask now, tucking one leg under me. "How come I never knew about any of this?"

She shrugs, like she's never really considered it. "Well, Grandpa and I got married. It's a pretty common story, I think. Your mom and her brothers needed me, and the rest of it . . ." She trails off. "Or that could just be excuses, of course. I guess there's no way to say for sure."

"Did you miss it?" I ask, picking the chocolate chips and cherries out of my granola bar before setting the rest of it down on a napkin. "Like, protesting?"

"Well, I suppose I was just protesting in different ways," she says thoughtfully. "Calling my senators, writing letters, donating money to causes I believed in. I was on a first-name basis with the staffers at Senator Kennedy's office back in the nineties." She looks at me meaningfully. "I like to think there are different ways of being a rebel. Doing what you can with what you have, and all of that."

"Wow," I say, shaking my head. "I had no idea."

"Well," she teases, "maybe you're not asking your old gram enough questions." She smiles. "Better do it now, while I can still remember the answers."

I frown. The idea that Gram won't always be here burns behind my ribs. "Gram," I start, but I think she can see that she rattled me, because she holds up one elegant hand.

"I'm just teasing, Marin-girl." She reaches out and squeezes my arm, then glances out the window; it's not quite so cold today, a surprising midwinter reprieve. "Now," she says, clapping her hands together. "You want to go for a walk to the bakery, see if we can get a halfway decent cookie?"

Do what you can with what you have, I remind myself firmly. "I'd love that," I say, snapping the lid back on the granola bars and standing up. Gram slips her hand into mine.

SEVENTEEN

The girls' volleyball championship is the following Wednesday, and weirdly people are actually talking about it. A couple of underclassmen have even told me they liked the piece I wrote about the school's glaring lack of support for the team.

"I feel like we should make a banner or something," Dave says, unwrapping his turkey sandwich at our table near the back of the cafeteria. The book club has been sitting together more lately—not every day, but a couple of times a week, which is nice considering Chloe seemingly wants nothing to do with me and otherwise I've been spending my lunch period in the library, working on my Title IX editorial.

"There are a bunch of supplies left over from the pep rally," Lydia puts in. She's a class rep for student council and always has the line on extra balloons or poster board or chocolate chip cookies floating around. "We could meet up after school."

I nod. "I've got my mom's car today," I say, smiling, as Lydia offers me one of her carrot sticks, "so I can drive some people over."

"No need," Gray says. "I got us a ride."

I turn to look at him. I hadn't even noticed him coming up behind me, and my skin prickles like it always does when I haven't had time to properly prepare for the sight of him. "What?"

He grins, all mischief. "You'll see. Just meet me out front after eighth period."

It's freezing outside when classes let out, the barren trees waving their branches at the far end of the parking lot and our breath visible in the chilly air. I find Gray with the rest of the book club over by the picnic tables at the side of the building; Gray is hard at work on a sign that reads, GO BRIDGEWATER, his bottom lip caught between his teeth as he concentrates.

"What?" he asks when he looks up and catches me smiling.

"Nothing," I say with a shake of my head. "Nice sign."

"Shut up," he says, blushing—blushing!—just the faintest bit. "Not all of us can be fancy, clever writer types."

"I'm not fancy," I assure him, though it's not like I'm mad about it.

"I think you're kind of fancy," Gray says.

I'm about to reply when a school bus pulls into the parking lot, the driver tooting the horn in cheery greeting.

"Oh, good," Gray says, putting the finishing touches on his sign and straightening up. "Our ride's here."

"Wait, what?" I blink at him. "You got us a . . . school bus?"

"I got us the lacrosse team's school bus," he admits, looking the slightest bit pleased with himself, "but there's a catch."

"And what's that?"

"We're not the only ones riding it over there." Gray nods at the gym entrance, and my eyes widen. The entire lacrosse team is trickling out of the locker room and toward the bus. Well, almost the entire lacrosse team—Jacob makes a point of scowling at me and walking off in the opposite direction.

"Seriously?" I gape at Gray. "You convinced them to come support?"

"They wanted to," Gray says, and I shoot him a dubious look. "Well, okay, maybe *wanted* to is the wrong way to put it, but still."

I laugh out loud as the rest of the club looks on in wonder. Even Ms. Klein looks surprised. "That's really decent of you, Gray."

"Well," he says. "I think you'll find that if you get to know me, I'm a pretty decent guy."

I open my mouth, not sure how to answer. He's not who I thought he was, that's for sure.

"You guys ready to load up?" Ms. Klein asks, saving me from my own awkward silence. I toss the leftover art supplies into the trunk of my mom's car and climb onto the bus, sliding into the empty seat beside Gray before I can talk myself out of it.

The game is at St. Brigid's, a fancy all-girls' school a couple of towns over, with floor-to-ceiling windows and state-of-the-art science labs. Gray heads over to the snack bar—an actual snack bar, not the crappy vending machines that are lined up outside our school—and comes back with a giant soda for himself and a bunch of bags of peanuts for everybody. "Are you, like, book club dad right now?" I ask, grinning as he passes them out.

"Maybe," he says. "Everybody needs to behave or I'll turn this volleyball game around, et cetera."

I snort, helping myself to a peanut. "You're kind of a nerd, huh? Is that, like, your big secret?"

Gray shrugs. "One of them," he admits, his eyes steady on mine. The back of his hand brushes mine. I can convince myself it's an accident until it happens again a few minutes later—the skate of his knuckles over my fingers, his pinky nearly hooking with mine. I bite my lip.

"Gray . . ."

He raises his eyebrows. "Marin," he says, exactly mimicking my tone.

I blow a breath out, debating. It's not that I'm not interested, obviously. If I'm being honest, I've been interested since the day of our first book club meeting, when he fixed the zipper on my backpack in the parking lot outside of school. Or before that, even. It's not like I never noticed him, always surrounded by admiring onlookers—it's just, I promised myself I'd never be one of them.

"You know what everybody says about girls when they hook up with you, right?" I ask him finally.

I'm expecting him to play dumb, but right away Gray nods. "I do know, actually," he says. "And it's fucked-up. I don't know why it's anybody's business. We're all just having a good time."

That surprises me, although probably it shouldn't. I'm guilty of it myself, aren't I? How many times did Chloe and I sit around on my front porch complaining about girls with the audacity to kiss boys we had crushes on, or how skanky some sophomore looked at the Valentine's Day dance? I have to admit, for all of Gray's alleged conquests, I've never heard a peep about him being anything less than gentlemanly to anyone. And I've certainly never heard him running his mouth.

"Anyway," he says now, cracking a peanut shell and offering me a cheeky smile. "Who says I'm trying to hook up with you to begin with?"

"I—" Suddenly I'm back at Bex's apartment: sure I misread the situation, confused his intentions. "I'm not saying—"

The panic must register on my face, because Gray nudges me gently in the shoulder. "I mean, no, I'm definitely trying to hook up with you," he admits. Then he shrugs. "But— and listen, I know this is going to sound like a line, and it's not—I'm not *only* trying to hook up with you, okay?"

I raise my eyebrows. "Oh no?"

"No," Gray says. "I meant what I said to you. I think

it's cool, what you're doing here. You kind of blow me away a little bit."

I consider that for a moment. I've spent the last few weeks feeling like such an outsider, it's hard to imagine Gray could think that what I'm doing is something cool. "Well," I say finally, "I will keep that in mind."

"You do that," Gray says, eyes warm and steady on me. "Now, if you'll excuse me, I'm trying to watch this volley-ball game."

I snort. "Oh, sorry, am I distracting you?"

"Yes, actually," he says, but he's grinning.

I can't help but grin back.

It's weird, watching the girls' volleyball team defend their title—after all, I know it's just a game. But something about it makes me feel hopeful, and when Elisa makes the winning point at the very end of the final set, the rest of us leap to our feet like lunatics, hooting as the ref blows his whistle and the team floods onto the court. Lydia and Dave are slapping each other five in all different configurations. Ms. Klein is screaming like a drunk football fan.

"Oh my god!" I fling my arms around Gray's neck before I totally know I'm going to do it, nearly knocking him clear off his feet, and when he ducks his head to kiss me, it feels like the most surprising win of all.

EIGHTEEN

Bex hands our response papers back the following morning.
I'm so prepared for an A that for a second I think that's what
I'm seeing before I realize there's actually a bright red *D* at
the top.

Wait, *what?*

I flip the paper over as fast as humanly possible, glancing around to make sure nobody saw it as my whole body
burns with shame and disbelief. I've never gotten a D in my
life, let alone on something that involved writing. Let alone
on something for *Bex*. It just . . . doesn't happen.

Except that apparently now it does.

We've got a vocab lesson this morning, but I barely hear anything anyone says the entire period over the horrified roar echoing inside my head. By the time class ends I've crafted an argument in my own defense worthy of Ruth Bader Ginsburg herself, but when I finally make it up to the front of the empty classroom all that comes out is a sputter.

"What happened?" I manage, holding the wrinkled paper out of in front of me, carefully typed pages drooping like so many white flags.

"I'm sorry, Marin," Bex says, looking disappointed. "But this essay just wasn't up to your usual standards."

"Wha—" I shake my head. "Why not?"

"It was rushed, and it was sloppy," he says. "It just felt like you didn't try at all. I know you've been spending a lot of time on your editorials. Maybe you've been distracted."

"That's not true," I say. "I mean, maybe it wasn't my best work. But seriously, a D?"

Bex just shrugs. "If you need to make it up, we can talk about extra credit."

Something about his attitude has the skin on the back of my neck prickling unpleasantly. This isn't about the essay. This feels personal.

"What is this really about?" I say.

"Excuse me?" Bex's eyebrows almost crawl off his face entirely.

"I don't deserve this grade. I just . . . I don't."

We both just stare at each other for a minute until Bex blows a breath out.

"What's up with you, huh?" he asks me, leaning back against his desk and scrubbing a hand through the hair at the back of his neck; for a moment he's the same Bex I recognize, whose class was my favorite part of the day.

That stops me. "What?"

"You've been a really tough crowd lately. With the reading list and your attitude in class . . . And you know, I didn't want to say this about your essays in the *Beacon*, but honestly . . ." He trails off.

I frown. "Honestly what?"

His eyes narrow. "I thought you said everything was cool."

I take a step back. "If everything was cool, would I not be getting a D on this paper?"

The words are out before I can think better of them. For a moment they hang there between us like a dare. Finally Bex presses his lips together, a muscle twitching once in his jaw.

"Easy, Marin," he says, and his voice is all warning. "I'm your teacher."

"Yeah," I say, shoving my useless paper into my backpack, turning around, and heading for the door. "I know."

I don't mention the paper to my parents. I don't know what stops me, exactly; I can't figure out who I'm protecting—me or Bex. It's my turn to clear the table after dinner that night, and I hold the plates distractedly under the faucet to rinse them, wondering if I made the smart move confronting him. Just once I'd like to be sure I was doing the right thing.

I stick the leftover cheese and sour cream back in the refrigerator—my dad made tacos tonight, Gracie loading hers up with enough jalapeños to have my eyes watering clear across the table—and wipe the counters with a slightly-grungy yellow sponge. My mom comes up behind me as I'm finishing up, resting her chin on my shoulder and wrapping her arms around my waist.

"Oh, hi there, daughter of mine," she says, squeezing gently. "I'm proud as hell of you, you know that?"

I glance at her out of the corner of my eye. I don't know how she senses when I need the extra encouragement. "Thanks."

"I mean it," she says, planting a kiss against my cheek before straightening up again. She gives the counter a perfunctory wipe with a dish towel, then glances at the clock on the stove. "*Grey's Anatomy* doesn't start for twenty minutes," she says thoughtfully. "You think that's enough time to run to Seven-Eleven for ice cream and get back?"

I consider it. "If we speed," I conclude after a moment.

My mom nods, scooping her keys off the hook near the doorway. "Let's go."

NINETEEN

Gray takes me skating at the Frog Pond on Boston Common on Friday night, his big hand warm against my chilly one as we weave our way through the crowded rink. Little kids in hockey skates whiz past clusters of college students in fur-collared parkas while Ariana Grande blasts over the speakers; a giant Christmas tree winks with colored lights.

Once the session ends we get hot chocolates in a tiny coffee shop overlooking the park, all Edison bulbs and basket-weave tile, a heavy velvet curtain hung across the doorway to keep out the chill. Gray folds his bulky body basically in half to sit in a wobbly chair by the window, his knees bumping the mosaic tabletop, which isn't much bigger than a dinner plate.

"You okay over there?" I ask with a laugh, grabbing my mug before its contents go sloshing over the sides.

"Oh, I'm great," he says, and I think he's joking around until I glance up and catch how he's looking at me, his gaze calm and steady. My whole body gets warm.

"Well," I say, taking a sip of my cocoa to hide my blush. I never felt like this with Jacob, like my actual bones were glowing deep inside my body just from being near him. "Good."

Gray breaks a massive snickerdoodle into two pieces, handing me half. "My moms make these every Christmas," he tells me. "They have this whole baking day they do—they both have a bunch of sisters, so my aunts and all my girl cousins come over and make like a million different kinds."

"And you taste test?" I joke.

Gray snorts. "You think my moms would let me get away with sitting on my ass while a bunch of womenfolk make me food?" he asks with a laugh. "I do my fair share. I'll have you know I'm an excellent measurer."

"I don't doubt that," I say with a smile. "So you have a big family?"

"Huge," Gray says, finishing his cookie in two bites. "Like, twenty-two first cousins. And some of them have kids now too. It's a zoo."

"That sounds nice," I tell him, using a teaspoon to scoop a mound of whipped cream out of my hot chocolate before it can sink to the bottom of the mug. "It's always just been Gracie and me and our parents. It's part of why we're so close to our gram."

"Oh yeah?" Gray looks interested. "Is she cool?"

"She's the best," I say immediately, leaving out the part where she's not always reliably herself these days. "And I actually just found out she's got this whole secret Riot Grrrl past I never knew about."

"That's awesome," Gray says with a grin.

We sit in the coffee shop for a long time, until the crowd thins out and it's just us and a glamorous-looking middle-aged woman nursing an espresso, and still I'm in no hurry to get home. Gray's a good question asker, full of self-deprecating stories about being the only guy in a family full of ladies; he's got a sister named Alice who's studying political science in Chicago.

"You guys will like each other," he says, totally confident, and I can't help but smile at his use of the future tense.

Finally the baristas start wiping down the tables in a

way that feels like a hint. We head out and make our way down Charles Street, our footsteps echoing on the cobblestones. Laughter spills out the doors of the bars. It should feel festive—Christmas break is only a few days away, and there are fairy lights and garlands strung up over the empty street—but out here in the cold and the dark I can feel the cloud of dread that's been following me around lately come sulking back. I'd forgotten about yesterday's conversation with Bex while Gray and I were hanging out—I'd forgotten about all of it, actually—but forgetting only works for so long. This whole thing is still a baffling, humiliating mess. God, what am I going to *do*?

Gray can tell something's up: he's been rambling cheerfully on, holding up the conversation for both of us, but as we tap our cards at the entrance to the brightly lit T station he pauses.

"Everything okay?" he asks, his cheeks gone pink from the cold. "It feels kind of like you just . . . went somewhere."

I shake my head. "It's nothing," I promise as we take the escalator to the elevated train platform, the dark expanse of the Charles River visible in the distance. The giant neon Citgo sign glows white and orange and blue. "It's dumb."

"It's nothing, or it's dumb?"

I hesitate. "Both?" I try, glancing down the track for

any sign of the train, even though the arrival board on the platform says we've got ten minutes to wait. "Neither?" I sigh, my breath just visible. "I don't know."

Gray nods, tucking his hands into his coat pockets. "You don't have to tell me jack shit, obviously," he says, rocking back on the heels of his boots. "But like, just FYI, you can if you want to. I get that this might come as a shock to you, but I'm actually a pretty good listener."

I snort, I can't help it. "You do realize that people who self-identify as good listeners are never actually good listeners, don't you?"

"Oh, really?" Gray shoots back, all mischief. "Did you come up with that theory while I was telling you my life story just now and you were like, reorganizing your sock drawer in your mind?"

"Rude!" I protest, elbowing him in the bicep. I tip my head back, look at the sky.

"Yeah, yeah," Gray says, dimples flashing. Then he shakes his head.

"Marin," he says, quiet enough that nobody else on the platform can hear him. "Try me."

I sigh, and then I just . . . tell him. I tell him everything—about Bex and about how Chloe has been so busy it feels sometimes like she's avoiding me and about lying to my parents and about the paper and the creeping feeling that somehow all of this is my fault.

"I don't want to get anybody in trouble," I finish finally, shivering a little inside my peacoat. "But I also feel like ignoring it hasn't made it go away so far."

Gray's quiet for a long time when I'm finished. Then all at once he shakes his head. "Holy shit, Marin," he says, and I'm surprised by how angry he sounds. "That dude is a total dick."

I bark a laugh, so loud and surprising that a woman looks at us curiously from the other side of the platform. All at once I realize it's what I was expecting Chloe to say when I told her. What I kind of *needed* for Chloe to say.

"Yeah," I reply, swallowing down that now-familiar tightness in my throat, that feeling of trying to keep it together. "I guess he kind of is."

"Not kind of," Gray says decisively. "A hundred percent."

I glance down at my boots on the concrete. "Do you think I should tell somebody?"

Gray thinks about that one for a moment. "I have no idea," he finally says, and he sounds very honest. "I think this is probably one of those times where my mom would say you have to decide what you can live with, which is seriously one of my least favorite mom-isms because it means there's no right answer." He shrugs. "But I can tell you I'll have your back no matter what you decide."

The train comes rumbling into the station then, fast and noisy. Gray reaches out and takes my hand.

TWENTY

I make an appointment to see Mr. DioGuardi during my free period on the Monday before Christmas break, perching on the very edge of his fake-leather visitor's chair and tucking my hands under my thighs to keep them from shaking. It's a small office, cluttered: the desk is heaped with file folders. A potted plant droops on the windowsill. There's a photo of Mr. DioGuardi's kids on the bookshelf, two college-aged guys with red hair and freckles clowning around at a campsite. A part of me can't help but wish he had a daughter too.

"Just, ah, give me one more second here," he says vaguely, holding up a finger and squinting at his computer screen; judging by the beeps and honks the thing has let out in the six minutes I've been sitting here, he's either attempting to hack into a government database or trying unsuccessfully to send an email attachment.

"Take your time," I say, though the truth is the longer he keeps me waiting the more I feel like I'm about to jump clear out of my skin and take off down the hallway, shedding muscle and viscera in my wake. I breathe in and force myself not to fidget. *Calm and quick*, I remind myself.

Finally Mr. DioGuardi folds his hands on top of his keyboard, frowning and jerking back as he hits the space bar by mistake. The computer dings in protest, and I bite the inside of my cheek to hold back a nervous giggle.

"So," he says. "Marin. What can I do for you?"

I take a deep breath. "Well—"

"I've been reading your editorials in the paper, by the way," he tells me, raising his eyebrows in a way that I'm not sure how to interpret, exactly. "I hadn't realized you had quite so much to say about the gender politics here at Bridgewater."

"Yeah." I muster a smile, cheerful and nonthreatening. "It's something I've been thinking about lately, I guess."

Mr. DioGuardi nods. "So it would seem." He clears his throat. "Now. What's on your mind?"

I swallow hard, digging my nails into my nylon-covered knees. "It's about Mr. Beckett," I admit.

"Oh?" Mr. DioGuardi's eyebrows twitch, cautious. "What about him?"

I take a deep breath and keep things as factual as possible, starting with the first day he drove me home and ending with the afternoon in his apartment.

"He kissed me," I say, cringing; God, I can't believe I'm using that word in front of Mr. DioGuardi. I can't believe I'm using that word about *Bex*. Everything about this is humiliating.

When I'm finished Mr. DioGuardi doesn't say anything for a long time, whistle clicking rhythmically against his two front teeth.

"These are serious allegations, Marin," he tells me finally. "You realize I'm required to report them to the school board. They'll want to do a full investigation."

"Okay," I say slowly, not sure if he's trying to warn me off or not. It kind of feels like maybe he is. "I just—what else is there to investigate?" I shake my head, confused. "I mean, I just told you what happened."

Mr. DioGuardi's impassive expression flickers, just barely. "Well, this is a process, Marin. We'll need to gather more information before we decide on a course of action.

They'll want to interview you themselves, first of all. And I imagine they'll want to speak to Mr. Beckett as well."

"And what if he says I'm making the whole thing up?"

Mr. DioGuardi frowns. "*Are* you?"

"What? No!" I say, more sharply than I mean to. "Of course not!"

"Watch the tone, please," Mr. DioGuardi reminds me, reaching for the whistle around his neck like he's checking to make sure it's still there in case he needs to foul me out. "I know this is an . . . emotional situation, which is exactly why there's a procedure in place." He smiles again—reassuring, dadlike. "These things take time, Marin. But the board will be thorough. You can trust us all to do our jobs."

I wrap my hands around the arms of the chair, knowing somehow—the way he said *emotional situation*, maybe— that there's no room to argue without proving his point.

"Okay," I say instead, reaching down for my backpack before standing up so quickly I get lightheaded. It's claustrophobic in here all of a sudden, the air too hot and thick to breathe properly. "Well. Um. Thank you. I should get back to class."

Mr. DioGuardi frowns. He was expecting me to be more grateful to him, I realize suddenly. And I'm not following the playbook.

"Marin—" he begins, but I paste another bland smile on my face before he can say anything else.

"I appreciate your help with this, Mr. DioGuardi." I promise. "Really."

"Of course," he says, mollified. I'm somebody he recognizes again: good student, reliable coeditor of the *Beacon*, not one to make a fuss. A nice girl.

"Feel free to come to my office with any questions. We're here to support you."

I thank him one more time, keeping the smile plastered on my face as I head out of his office. I wave to Ms. Lynch, who's scrolling industriously through Facebook on her office computer. I wait until I'm out in the empty hallway to let the mask slip off my face, leaning against a bank of sophomore lockers and taking deep breaths, trying to swallow down the whirlpool of dread rising in my chest. I wanted telling Mr. DioGuardi to put an end to this whole miserable episode.

But now it looks like it's barely begun.

Gray's waiting by my locker at the end of last period, tie already loosened and a charmingly ridiculous reindeer beanie—complete with pompom—shoved down over his wavy hair.

161

"Hey," he says, with a smile that makes me shiver in spite of the sense of impending doom I've been carting around since my meeting with DioGuardi. "How did it go?"

I shrug. "Okay, I guess?" I fill him in as quickly and factually as possible, trying not to sound like a person at the mercy of her own *emotional situation*. "It sounds like I'll know more after the break."

"Well, that's good, right?" Gray asks. "That he's bringing it to the school board?"

"No, it is," I agree, though in fact the very idea makes me want to dig a hole in the nearest snowbank and live inside it till spring. Already I feel like an idiot for having ever imagined I could tell my story to DioGuardi and that would be the end of it. It feels like a theme in my life lately: what did I *think* was going to happen? "It is."

"Good," Gray says again, like it's just that simple; still, I know he's just trying to be encouraging. "You coming to pizza?"

I shake my head. Everybody at Bridgewater always goes for slices at Antonio's on the last day of school before Christmas break; normally it's one of my favorite afternoons of the year, the line spilling out onto the chilly sidewalk and the smell of cheese and pepperoni warm in the air. Today, though, I can't face the thought of being around that many people. "There's something I gotta do," is all I say.

My mom is working on her laptop at the dining room table when I get home, paperwork spread out in messy piles all around her; my dad is already prepping the Feast of the Seven Fishes for Christmas Eve tomorrow night.

"Hey, guys?" I say, setting my backpack down in the mudroom, tucking my hair behind my ears. I steel myself against the panicky feeling of having set a series of events into motion, when I'm not even sure it was the right thing to do. "I think we probably need to have a talk."

TWENTY-ONE

I'm expecting fireworks from my mom in particular—
after all, this is the same woman who marched down the
street in her pajamas and put the fear of god in Avery
Demetrios when she was mean to me at day camp the summer after fourth grade—but instead she just sits stock-still
at the table and listens, one hand in my father's and one
hand in mine.

"He did *what*?" she asks when I get to the part about the
kiss, but my dad's grip tightens around her fingers, and she
immediately presses her lips together.

"I'm sorry," she says, shaking her head like she's trying

to clear it, and I see her eyes getting watery. "Keep going."

So I do, staring down at the table and telling them about my editorial and the response paper and ending with today and my conversation with Mr. DioGuardi. When I'm finished all three of us are quiet for a long moment.

"God*damnit*, Marin," my mom says, and when I look up at her I'm surprised to see she's wiping tears away with her whole palm. "I am so, so sorry he did that to you."

We sit at the table for a long time, all three of us talking. My dad makes us a snack of cheese and crackers and grapes. They don't ask any of the questions I'm expecting: *Are you sure you weren't confused? Did you give him the wrong impression? What the hell were you doing in his apartment to begin with?* I don't know why I feel a tiny bit guilty about that, like maybe they're letting me off too easy.

All of us startle when the back door opens and Gracie ambles through, back from her carpool with her cheeks gone pink from the cold.

"I'm starving," she announces, then registers all three of us sitting around the table like we're conducting a séance. "What's wrong?"

I hesitate for a moment, then take a breath and smile. "Nothing," I promise, offering her a cracker; sitting here between my parents it feels like maybe it could be the truth.

"Everything's okay."

I go to Chloe's the day after Christmas, pulling my mom's car into the driveway and skirting past the enormous blow-up snow globe on her parents' front lawn. Every year the two of them get more and more into the holidays, three-foot-tall candy canes lining the flower beds and a motorized, light-up Santa waving from beside the chimney. To Chloe it's the literal most embarrassing thing on the planet—none of our other friends are allowed to come over between Thanksgiving and New Year's—but I've always thought it was kind of great.

Once her mom lets me in I wave to Chloe's brothers, who are sprawled on the carpet in front of the Christmas tree playing Battleship, and find Chloe still in her pajamas in her bedroom, watching an eyeliner tutorial on her laptop.

"Hey," she says, looking surprised when I knock on the mostly closed door.

I frown. "We're doing the mall, aren't we?" Chloe and I have done the mall the day after Christmas for the last four years, returning ugly sweaters from our various family members and taking advantage of the clearance sales. We always end with a peppermint mocha at the scruffy hipster coffee shop in Inman Square.

"Oh." Chloe shakes her head, like this is totally new information and not something we've been doing since before we got our periods. "Yeah, I guess. I don't know. I just figured you'd be with Gray."

"What?" I shake my head. I didn't even realize she knew about me and Gray, and it stings to think how little we've been hanging out. "Gray's in New Hampshire with his cousins until New Year's. But also, why would I be with Gray? This is our day, right?"

"Right." Chloe shrugs. "I don't know."

I frown. "Do you not want to go?" I mean, obviously I know things have been weird with us, and I don't 100 percent believe all the time she's been spending with Kyra, but it would just be so much weirder to *not* do this.

"No, we can," she says, shutting her laptop with a look on her face like I just invited her for a rousing afternoon of digging a hole in the frozen earth. "I just have to shower."

"I mean, we don't have to." Suddenly it does feel like a bad idea, actually: Chloe's lousy mood, yeah, but also the crowds, the chance of running into people we know from school. Running into *Bex*. I sit down on the edge of her unmade bed.

"Can I tell you something?" I ask, picking at a loose thread in the quilt her mom made out of all her old day camp

T-shirts. "Without you, like, freaking out?"

Chloe raises her eyebrows. "Is it that you got Bex in trouble with DioGuardi?" she asks immediately.

"I—" My eyes widen. "How do you know that?"

"Everybody knows that," Chloe says, sliding the laptop onto the mattress and climbing out of bed. "Like, the entire school."

"What? Seriously?" My heart drops. I purposely talked to Mr. DioGuardi on the last day before vacation to buy myself time before the gossip mill started grinding. "How?"

Chloe shrugs. "I have no idea," she says, though she's not quite looking at me.

"Well, I mean, who told *you*?"

"Does it matter?"

"I mean, yeah, Chloe. If people are going around saying—"

"Can you stop messing with that?" she interrupts, nodding at the quilt. "The whole thing is going to fall apart any second."

"Sorry." I set it down, wiping my suddenly sweaty palms on the knees of my jeans. "Are you mad at me?" I ask, although the answer is pretty obvious. What I can't figure out is the why.

Chloe scoops her bathrobe off the back of the closet

door, draping it over her arm. "I just don't understand why you even bothered asking what I thought you should do," she says, shrugging inside her Bridgewater hoodie. "When, like, you obviously had your own agenda this whole entire time."

"Wait, wait, wait," I protest. "I don't have an agenda. What does that even mean?"

Chloe huffs like I'm being dense on purpose. "It means you, like, decided you had this vendetta against him, and now—"

"Against *Bex*?" I shake my head. "That's not even—"

"You know he's probably going to get fired, right?" Chloe cuts in. "And we'll be stuck with some hundred-year-old sub for the rest of the year who's going to make us read a bunch of boring crap and write, like, detailed sequence-of-events responses, just because you couldn't drop the rock about some dumb misunderstanding."

"Holy shit, Chloe." I feel my throat get tight, my eyes stinging; in the whole entire history of our friendship, she's never talked to me like this before. "What the hell is your problem?"

"I don't have a problem," Chloe snaps; then, looking over her shoulder at the hallway, she lowers her voice. "I just don't understand why you're being like this, that's all.

Like, why can't you just admit you made a mistake—"

"I didn't make a mistake!"

"So what, you think he's in love with you?" Chloe laughs meanly. "Like he brought you to his apartment as part of some super-secret plan to make you his girlfriend?"

"No, of course not." My eyes are filling for real now, my vision blurring. I glance up at the overhead light, take a deep breath. "You realize you're supposed to be my best friend."

"I *am* your best friend," Chloe says immediately. "And part of my job is to tell you when you're making a total fool of yourself."

"Is that what you think I'm doing?"

"I think you've lost all connection with reality, yeah."

"Well . . ." And I shrug, because what else can you say to that? I stand up and sling my bag over my shoulder, wiping my face with the heel of my hand. "I guess today's not such a good mall day after all."

"No," Chloe says, still clutching her bathrobe in front of her like a shield. "I guess not."

I head downstairs and let myself out, dodging her mom in the kitchen. The boys are still playing in the living room, their trash talk just audible over the clatter of the Cartoon Network.

"Sunk!" one of them says, gleeful. The sound of them laughing is the last thing I hear before I shut the door.

TWENTY-TWO

My parents and I meet with Principal DioGuardi and the school board over break, all of us sitting around a folding table on the stage in the auditorium. I wonder if they made Mr. Lyle come in specifically to set it up. I give the board my full statement, feeling weirdly like I'm performing in a play I never auditioned for; they assure us that they're taking the matter very seriously, that they'll be talking to Mr. Beckett as well.

The rest of Christmas vacation is achingly quiet. Gray gets back from New Hampshire and takes me to breakfast at Deluxe Town Diner. Gracie and I go see *The Nutcracker* with my mom. My dad sits through about a million Hallmark Christmas movies without complaining, getting up periodically to get us more homemade marshmallow hot chocolate cookies, which I know is code for *I love you and I'm here.*

My mom lets me take her car in my first morning back after break, the security blanket of knowing I could make a quick exit if I needed to. I slam the driver's door shut before dashing across the parking lot, the pavement sleet-slippery under my boots. Icy rain slides underneath the collar of my winter coat, and I almost wipe out hard on the concrete staircase, catching myself on the railing just in time.

I shake my hair out once I make it through the senior entrance and scan the bright, crowded hallway. Harper Russo raises her eyebrows, then whispers something to Kaylin Benedetto. Michael Cyr shoots me a giant, shit-eating grin.

I duck my face and head for my locker, telling myself I'm being dramatic—this is my actual high school, not the establishing shot of a nineties teen movie. Still, I grab my books as quickly as humanly possible, edging past Cara St. John and Aminah Thomas in the bottleneck in the hallway.

"—always hanging out with him in the newspaper office," Cara is saying, scooping her shoulder-length hair into a stubby blond ponytail. "I don't know what she thought was going on."

"I *wish* Bex would try something with me," Aminah chimes in with a snort, then happens to glance over her shoulder and spot me right behind her. The embarrassment on her face is nothing compared to the hot, prickly wave of nausea that rolls through my entire body.

So. Everybody really does know, then.

I shuffle dazedly through my first two classes, feeling like my head has been wrapped in gauze and I can't see or hear or even breathe properly. All morning I try to imagine what I'll do if Bex is in his classroom at the start of AP English, and all morning I try to imagine what I'll do if he's not.

"You ready?" Gray asks, slipping his hand into mine as we head down the hallway, and I nod.

I've been telling myself I'll be fine no matter what happens, but I can't deny the way my knees go wobbly with relief when I see the sub standing up in front of Bex's classroom, a nerdy-looking middle-aged guy with a comb-over and a paunch.

"Nice," Gray murmurs, a smile spreading over his face as we take our seats. "See? Dude's gone. Nothing to worry about."

"Yeah." I muster a small smile of my own. It falls as

Chloe comes in, stopping short at the sight of the sub.

"Hey," I say quietly, as she passes by my desk. "Can we talk?"

Chloe ignores me.

The sub introduces himself as Mr. Haddock—"like the fish," he clarifies, looking visibly pained when nobody laughs—and launches into this week's vocab lesson. He's dry as toast and just as achingly boring as Chloe predicted. But I don't care at all.

Apparently, I'm the only one.

"This guy suuucks," Dean Shepherd mutters from the back of the room.

"At least Marin won't try to screw him," Michael Cyr cracks in response. "I mean . . . probably."

I stare fire down at my notes, my face flaming. Gray fixes them both with a look.

"Excuse me?" Chloe pipes up at the front of the room, raising her hand primly. "When will Mr. Beckett be back?"

Mr. Haddock frowns. "He should be here tomorrow, I believe—but I have no intention of wasting the time I've got with you folks, so if you'll open your books—"

I lose the rest of what he says underneath the sudden roar in my head. For a moment I honestly think I've heard him wrong.

Tomorrow. He'll be back . . . tomorrow?

God, I'm such an idiot.

This isn't finished at all.

Once the bell finally rings I'm out of my seat like a sprinter at the starting gun, ignoring Gray as he heads toward me and stumbling down the hall toward the admin suite, where Ms. Lynch is eating a bag of Famous Amos cookies and hungrily scrolling a gossip site on her computer. "Is Mr. DioGuardi here?" I blurt.

Her eyes narrow. "Excuse you," she says, quickly minimizing the window; I wouldn't have pegged her for a Rihanna fan, but I guess we all contain multitudes. I can't wait to tell Chloe, until I remember Chloe and I aren't speaking.

"Do you have an appointment?"

You keep his calendar, I think but don't say. *You know I don't.*

"Um, nope," I manage, aiming for bright and winding up somewhere in the neighborhood of totally deranged. "Just a quick social call."

Ms. Lynch frowns. "I'll tell him you're here."

I take a seat in the outer office to wait, watching the seconds tick by on the ancient clock out in the hallway. It's the better part of ten minutes before the door opens and Mr. DioGuardi comes out.

"Marin!" he says, looking not at all pleased to see me. "Come on in. You were on my list of students to touch base with this morning."

I bet I was, I think bitterly.

"Mr. Beckett is coming back tomorrow?"

Mr. DioGuardi frowns. "Have a seat," he says, gesturing to the chair across from him. "That's what I wanted to talk to you about. The school board investigated your . . . allegations over the break. Ultimately, the disciplinary committee found no conclusive evidence of wrongdoing, so he'll be returning to his classes for the remainder of the year."

"I *told* you about the wrongdoing," I say, and it comes out a lot more like a wail than I mean for it to. I swallow hard, digging my nails into the armrests. *Don't be hysterical. Don't be a crazy girl.* "I just mean—"

"I understand that, Marin," Mr. DioGuardi says. "But without any corroborating statements, without evidence—"

"No evidence—" I break off as the larger implications here start to make themselves clear. "So you think I'm *lying?*"

"Now hold on just a moment," he says. "No one is saying that."

"Well then what *are* you saying?"

"Marin—" Mr. DioGuardi pops his whistle into his

mouth for a moment, then pulls it out again. When he speaks his voice is suddenly gentle.

"Look," he says, "is it at all possible you misinterpreted what was happening? With Mr. Beckett, I mean? No one would blame you, obviously. He's one of our younger faculty members, and I see so many girls hanging around his classroom, or in the newspaper office. It would be perfectly understandable if you somehow misunderstood—"

"Oh my god." It's out before I can stop it. I shove my chair back and jump upright. "I'm not listening to this."

Mr. DioGuardi's eyes narrow across the desk. "Marin," he says sharply. "I understand you're upset, but may I remind you who you're talking—"

Stop using my name, I want to scream loud enough to shatter the windows. Instead, I press my lips together, remembering my manners. Swallowing down my own rage and fear.

"You're right," I manage, the words like gravel in my mouth. I hold my hands up, forcing a cowed smile. "I'm sorry. I shouldn't have—you're right."

Mr. DioGuardi nods with a thin smile—pleased, I think, to be in the position of being able to give me a pass in this trying time. "All I mean is that these things happen," he continues. "And sometimes, once we've had time to cool

177

off and reconsider a situation from all angles, we find we see things differently than we might have at first."

"Sure," I say. I focus on the bookcase, on that photo of DioGuardi's sons at the campsite. I want to rip it off the shelf and hurl it directly at his head, then encourage him to take some time to cool off and reconsider the situation from all angles. "I get it."

"Now," he says, standing himself, "if you don't have any further questions——?"

"Um, nope," I say, backing up toward the doorway. What else could there possibly be to ask? "I guess that's it. Thanks for letting me know."

"Of course," Mr. DioGuardi says, and his smile is genuine relief as he shuffles me out into the admin suite. "I'm glad we had this talk."

TWENTY-THREE

"This is un-frickin'-acceptable," my mom announces that night, slamming pots and pans around the kitchen like she's thinking of starting a percussion ensemble.

"I mean it. I've had it. I'm going to march in there and stick my boot so far up that man's ass that he'll be able to open up his mouth and read the L.L.Bean logo in the mirror. Then I'm calling a lawyer."

"Dyana," my dad says from his perch at the kitchen table, sounding faintly weary. I cringe at the sight of the bags under his eyes. "Go easy, will you?"

"You go easy!" my mother snaps, yanking open the

fridge and brandishing a Styrofoam package of ground turkey like a weapon. "This is ridiculous. And frankly I don't think there's anything wrong with showing our daughter it's okay to get worked up over injustices." She drops the turkey in the pan with a wet thud. "Which this is."

"Nobody's saying it isn't an injustice," my dad puts in, getting up to check the potatoes in the oven. "I'm just saying that I don't see how violence is going to help—"

"It's metaphorical violence, Dan." My mom makes a face as she jabs at the turkey with a wooden spoon. "Mostly."

"Guys," I protest weakly. "Please. I can handle this."

My dad scrubs a hand over his face. "Can you transfer out of the class?" he asks me. "I feel like that should be the first step, right?"

I bite the end off a baby carrot and think about that for a minute, surprised by how simple he makes it sound. And it *would* be simple, really: there's a non-AP senior English class that meets at the same time, two rooms over. They're reading *The Art of Fielding*. It would probably be fine.

I take a deep breath. "No," I tell them, calm as I can manage.

My mom raises one thick brow. "Why not?"

I shrug, popping the rest of the carrot into my mouth

and crunching hard. "Because then he wins."

My parents are both quiet then, the two of them exchanging a look across the kitchen. I think it might be worry. I think it might be pride. My mom sets the wooden spoon down on the counter, then comes over and slides an arm around my waist.

"Go get your sister," she says, squeezing once before letting me go. "It's almost time to eat."

I'm finishing up some homework later that night when Gracie gallops down the hallway, grabbing hold of the doorjamb and swinging her gangly body into my room. Her nails are painted a bright, sparkly blue. "There's a boy here for you," she reports.

"What?" I had my earbuds jammed into my ears in an attempt to block out the rest of the world entirely. I didn't even hear the doorbell ring. "Seriously?"

"Yep," Gracie says, popping the *P* delightedly. "And he's hot."

"Oh God." I check my hair in the mirror—end-of-the-day greasy, but there's nothing to be done about it now—then slick on some ChapStick and head downstairs.

Gray is standing near the front door, his hands shoved into the pockets of his oversize sweatpants as he chats gamely to my parents about *We Should All Be Feminists,* which we're going to be discussing at book club on Thursday. My mom looks completely enamored. My dad looks completely confused.

"So," I say brightly. "You've met Gray."

My mom raises her eyebrows. "We have," she tells me, in a voice that unmistakably communicates the fact that up until this moment I've entirely failed to mention him. *I didn't think he was for real,* I want to explain to her, although looking at him standing here like a friendly giant in my parents' tiny foyer it occurs to me again how wrong I was.

My mom looks like she'd be more than happy to settle in and spend the rest of the evening with Gray watching Chimamanda Ngozi Adichie's TED Talk, but thankfully my dad lays a hand on her arm.

"We were just about to head upstairs," he says. "There's ice cream in the freezer, if you kids are interested."

"Sorry," Gray says, making a face once it's just the two of us in the foyer. "Is this okay? I didn't mean to get you in trouble or anything like that."

"Oh, no, you're fine." I shake my head. "They're not those kind of parents." They are, however, the kind of parents who are probably lurking around the corner hoping to accidentally-on-purpose overhear us, so I grab my coat off the overflowing rack, zipping it over my leggings and Bridgewater hoodie and leading Gray out onto the porch.

"So what's up?" I say, tucking my hands into my pockets and shivering a little; January in Massachusetts is brutal, single-digit temperatures and the kind of shrieking wind that chaps your face and stings the insides of your ears. "Everything okay?"

"Yeah, totally." Gray shrugs. "I just wanted to check on you, I guess. I mean, not that you can't take care of yourself or anything, but I wanted to make sure you were hanging in there after . . ." He trails off, a little awkwardly. "You know. After."

I raise my eyebrows and smile. "You could have done that over text," I point out.

Gray nods. "I could have," he agrees. "I didn't want to."

"Oh no?" I'm grinning for real now, I can't help it. I've never met anyone like him before. "Why not?"

Gray's fingertips brush the hem of my coat, just lightly. "You know why not."

"Well. I'm glad you did." I look down at my fuzzy slippers, suddenly shy. "I'm okay, I guess. I feel a little bit like I just made the biggest mistake of my life, possibly? But other than that, super."

"It wasn't a mistake," Gray says immediately. "I mean,

easy for me to say, right? But I don't think it's ever a mistake to tell the truth."

It *is* easy for him to say, probably. Still, I appreciate the sentiment.

"Maybe not," I allow. But then I think of the look on Chloe's face this morning, the whispers that followed me down the hallway. "It just feels like the truth didn't mean anything, you know? Like I put myself out there, I opened myself up to all this shit, everybody staring at me and making their judgments, and it didn't even change anything."

Gray considers that. "Maybe not," he says quietly. "But it kind of changed you, right?"

That stops me; I'm quiet for a moment, turning it over in my mind. On one hand, there's no silver lining here—it's not like I'm *glad* this all happened, but I guess it's true that I'm tougher than I was a couple of months ago. It's true that I see things differently now.

"Maybe," I say again, shivering a little in the bitter cold.

"Come here," Gray says quietly; for a moment I think he's going to kiss me, but in the end he just wraps me in his arms. We stand there for a long time in the glow of the porch light, the winter wind calling down the empty street.

TWENTY-FOUR

I barely sleep that night, picking half-heartedly at an Eggo on my ride to school the following morning and letting my coffee go cold in the cup holder. I may have been ready to raise hell in the kitchen of my parents' house last night, but this morning all I want is to run right out the door and disappear into the woods behind the football field. Forget switching classes, I think miserably. At this point I'm ready to try homeschooling for the rest of the year.

Gray finds me in the hallway before third period. "Hey," he says, reaching for my hand and squeezing. "How you doing?"

"Me?" I paste the world's fakest smile on my face, then realize it's just Gray and let it melt into an exaggerated grimace, crossing my eyes and baring my teeth. "I'm super. Why, do I not look super?"

"Oh, no, totally super," Gray says grandly, bumping his shoulder against mine before we head inside and take our seats. I tell myself I'm imagining the low murmurs as I make my way down the aisle. Chloe, meanwhile, will barely look at me.

"Hey," I try, kicking lightly at her chair from across the aisle; she offers me a smile even faker than the one I tried on Gray a minute ago, then turns back to her bullet journal. I sigh and pull my notebook out of my bag.

Bex isn't in class by the time the bell rings for the start of the class period. For a second I let myself hope for dorky Mr. Haddock, but a moment later Bex strolls through the door with his reusable coffee cup in hand, like possibly he was lurking outside in the hallway just waiting for the exact right time to make his entrance.

"There he is," Dean calls, slouched in his chair near the window. "Thought you abandoned us, man."

Bex flashes the dimple in his cheek, easy. "Me?" he asks, all innocence. "Never."

He's wearing dark khakis and one of his signature

chambray shirts, a fresh new haircut that makes him look even younger than usual.

"Now, tell me: did you guys manage to actually learn anything yesterday, or not so much?"

He takes attendance and asks if anybody's read anything good lately, just like always, then opens up a detailed discussion of some Joyce story with absolutely no fanfare whatsoever. The weirdest part is how into it everyone gets—Dean Shepherd offers surprising insight into the story's symbolism. Chloe raises her hand about a thousand times. I don't know what I was expecting, but it wasn't this: it's like he's going to make things normal again through sheer force of will, and everybody has decided to go along with it. It makes me feel more than a little crazy. More than that though, I'm *furious*—the kind of anger that could light fires and power cities, the kind that laughs at the limits of my nice-girl self-control. *Why doesn't anybody care about what happened?* I want to shriek, loud enough to rattle the windows. *Why doesn't anybody care about* me?

I scribble in the margins of my notebook and pray he doesn't call on me to make some kind of point about how fine everything is between us. It feels like years before the end of the period.

"All right, that's it for today," he says as the bell rings.

"Marin, can you stay after for a sec? Yeah, yeah," he says, shaking his head at the assorted snorts and snickers from the back of the room. "Get out of here, the rest of you animals."

I startle at that, gaping at Bex as everyone files out of the classroom—everyone, that is, except Gray, who leans against the doorjamb, backpack slung over one broad shoulder like he's waiting for the public bus.

"What are you doing?" I ask, my gaze darting from him to Bex and back again.

"I'm gonna stay," he announces.

"I'm fine," I lie. "Go."

Gray shakes his head. He's taller than Bex, and broader; he fills almost the whole doorway. "Nah, I'm good here."

I know he means well, but it feels like he's peeing a circle around me.

"Go," I tell him through gritted teeth. "Gray, seriously."

Gray goes, but not before shooting Bex a look that could take the bark right off a tree. "See you at lunch, Marin," he says.

Bex watches him go for a moment before turning back to me. "Well!" he says, faux-brightly, and there's that sheepish smile again. "I guess we know where I stand with your friend Gray."

I take a step backward; the backs of my legs bump

awkwardly against a desk. "He's just—"

"I'm kidding," Bex says, holding both hands up. "It was a joke." Then he makes a face.

"Okay," he says, perching on the edge of his desk, "Marin. Can we just . . . reset?"

"Reset?" I repeat dumbly. That . . . is not what I was expecting him to say. "Like . . . between us?"

"Yeah," Bex says. He picks a rubber band up off his desk, stretching it between his thumbs. "Listen, I'm sorry I came down so hard on you about that paper."

Wait, *what?*

"It wasn't about the paper," I blurt, faintly horrified. Holy shit, is that what he thinks? "I mean, I didn't go to Mr. DioGuardi just because—"

"No, no, no, of course not," Bex says. He's still fidgeting with the rubber band. "That's not what I'm saying."

Then what are *you saying?* I want to ask, but even as I have the thought it feels extremely unwise to argue. I think of the way everyone's been staring at me since yesterday morning. I think of Mr. DioGuardi and *maybe you were confused*.

"Okay," I say finally, edging toward the doorway. My heart is thudding. "Yeah. Um. A reset would be great."

"Good," Bex says, finally dropping the rubber band

back into a jar on the desk and getting to his feet. "Glad to hear it."

"Okay," I say again. "Um. Thanks."

"No problem," he says, with a brisk, businesslike nod. "Have a good day."

I pull my backpack up on my shoulder and book it out of Bex's classroom. Gray's leaning cross-ankled against a bank of lockers across the hall.

"How'd it go?" he asks, standing upright and reaching for my hand.

I shrug, weirdly reluctant to talk about it. "Fine?"

"Fine like he's going to move to Saskatchewan and never talk to you again?"

"No, fine like . . ." I shake my head, fighting a flash of annoyance. I know he's just trying to be supportive, but I need a second to myself to try to figure out what just happened. "Forget it."

"No, hey, talk to me." Gray puts a hand on my arm, but I shrug him off, harder than I mean to. He takes a step back, hands up.

"Sorry." I feel like a shaken-up soda bottle, like if anyone even looks at me wrong I might explode in every direction. "I think I just need some air."

"Marin—" Gray frowns. "You're not coming to lunch?"

I shake my head. "Not hungry," I say. "I'll see you later, okay?" I don't wait for him to answer as I head down the hallway.

I'm so focused on getting away from him—on getting away from everyone—that I've made it almost all the way to the far end of the building before I realize I have no idea where I'm actually headed. It feels like there's nowhere to hide. Two months ago I would have hightailed it directly to the newspaper room, flung myself down on the couch—and complained at great length to Bex himself, probably. It's grossly surprising to realize I miss him—or at least, I miss the person I thought he was. All at once I'm furious he's taken that from me too.

Finally I make my way to the bio lab, where Ms. Klein is sitting at her desk grading papers and eating peanut butter out of the jar with a spoon.

"Hey, Marin," she says, surprise flickering briefly over her features. "You okay?"

"Yep!" I say. "I just, um—" I break off, trying to come up with some kind of plausible book-club-related excuse for being in here and coming up empty.

Ms. Klein doesn't seem to need one: "Do you want to talk?" she asks quietly, putting down her pen. "About . . . what everyone is talking about?"

"Um," I say, struggling to keep my voice even. God, I can't believe even Ms. Klein knows. "Not really. Can I just, like, hang out in here for a bit?"

Ms. Klein lifts her chin in the direction of the lab benches. "Sure thing," she says, and her voice is very even. "Have a seat."

TWENTY-FIVE

Weekend afternoons are notoriously slow at Niko's if there isn't a bridal shower or a Christening booked in the sunroom, which is bad news for tips but good news in that it'll give me four long, boring hours' worth of chances to try and smooth things over with Chloe. We've been avoiding each other since we got back from break—or, more to the point, Chloe's been avoiding me. On the rare occasions I've made it into the cafeteria, she's been eating with some girls from the drama club. We've been putting the next issue of the *Beacon* together entirely via a string of extremely tense, polite emails.

When I get to the restaurant though, I find Chloe's monosyllabic cousin Rosie rolling silverware at the wait station instead, chunky rings on every one of her fingers and a diamond stud glittering in her nose.

"She changed up her schedule," Steve explains when I ask about it, looking vaguely uncomfortable. "Some new club she's in."

I sincerely doubt that—after all, it's Saturday—but it's not like I'm about to argue with her dad of all people. I shuffle my way through my shift, then swing by Sunrise with two plastic clamshells of baklava tucked under my arm. I drop one with Camille at the nursing station and bring the other into Gram's room, where we sit on the love seat with the window cracked to let a tiny bit of cold, fresh air in, brushing flakes of puff pastry off our laps.

"Oh, you know what, Marin?" she says suddenly, getting up off the sofa and heading for the closet, surprisingly spry in her cardigan and khakis. "I've got something for you."

I raise my eyebrows, surprised. "You do?"

"I do!" She stands on her tiptoes and rummages along the top shelves for a moment; when she turns around she's holding a fabric-covered storage box, the kind you buy at craft supply stores. We must have moved a hundred of them from her house in Brockton, full of old papers and mementos and slightly creepy locks of hair from when my mom and uncles were little kids. When she brings this one back to the love seat and pulls the top off though, I see it's full of old photos—and not the ones from the seventies that I'm used to seeing, my mom with pigtails riding her bike and my uncles' hair curling down over their collars. These are older: my grandpa at his high school graduation, looking grave and serious even as a teenager. The narrow brick apartment building in the North End where my grandma grew up. And—

"Is that *you?*" I ask, grabbing a faded photo out of the pile and holding it up to get a better look.

"Damn right it's me," Gram says with a laugh. Her shiny brown hair is longer than I've ever seen it. She's standing in a crowd in a leafy green park, dressed in bell-bottoms and huge sunglasses and a sleeveless white T-shirt, a clunky beaded necklace nestled in the deep V of the collar. She looks ferocious, her arms flung in the air and her mouth opened in a howl.

"What is— I mean, what are you—" I break off, not even sure which question to start with. "Is this in the city?" I finally ask.

She nods. "Right on Boston Common," she says. "I

took the bus in with a bunch of girlfriends for a civil rights demonstration. Your grandfather almost lost his mind."

"He didn't want you to protest?" I ask, eyebrows raised.

"Well, I wouldn't say *that*, exactly." Gram takes the picture from my hand, gazes at it appraisingly. "But he was worried about me, I think."

"Well, if this was when you got arrested, I guess he was right to be."

Gram waves a hand. "Oh, please," she says with a smirk. "First of all, this wasn't the protest where I got arrested. Second of all, maybe worried isn't the right way to put it. We were coming from different places, that's all. He didn't always understand why certain things were important to me, or why I reacted to things the way I did." She smiles at the picture, almost to herself. "He tried though. And that was the most important thing."

I think of Gray then. He and I haven't talked much either, the last couple of days, and I feel crummy about the way we left things outside Bex's classroom. I know he just wanted to take care of me, back in Bex's classroom. I didn't know how to explain how important it felt for me to take care of myself.

I'm about to ask Gram what she thinks I should do about him when Camille knocks on the door, poking her head in.

"That baklava is delicious," she reports with a smile. "How are you ladies doing in here?"

"We're great," Gram says, beaming, the box of photos still balanced in her narrow lap. "My daughter is visiting."

"Granddaughter," I remind her gently.

"Of course," Gram says. "My granddaughter. Ah . . ." She trails off then, a flash of panic skittering across her face; I can see she's lost her train of thought.

"Marin," I say, trying to keep my voice casual. She's never forgotten my name before. It's a fluke, that's all. "But Camille and I know each other already, remember?"

"We're old friends," Camille says. She's smiling, but her tone is slightly wary, her gaze flicking from me to Gram and back again. "You girls just yell if you need me, okay?"

"We will," I promise, and smile back.

I'm waiting in the bio lab Monday morning before first period when Gray appears in the doorway, looking around the empty room and back at me with confusion written all over his face. "Hey," he says. "Am I early?"

I shake my head. "Nope," I promise. "Right on time."

Gray nods slowly. "There was a note taped to my locker this morning," he says, the faintest of smirks appearing at the very edges of his mouth. "Said there was an emergency book club meeting before first period. You wouldn't happen to know anything about that, would you?"

I tilt my head to the side for a moment, pretending to consider. "It's possible," I admit, holding up the Dunkin' Donuts box I picked up on the way in this morning, "that you're pretty much looking at it."

"Ah." Gray smiles a real smile now, all straight white teeth and sheepish expression. "You know, as I was coming over here I was wondering what the hell an emergency book club meeting could possibly be about. But I figured, what do I know, right? I'm new."

"There could conceivably have been some time-sensitive literary issue," I protest with a laugh. Then I shake my head. "I'm sorry I lost it like that the other day," I tell him. "Outside Bex's classroom."

Gray snorts. "That was you losing it?" he asks, sitting down on the sagging sofa beside me.

I shrug. "You know what I mean."

Gray nods. "You can tell me, you know," he says, leaning his head back against the threadbare cushions. "If you need space. I know I can be, like, a lot sometimes. Just say, 'Gray, with respect, go fuck off.' Easy as that."

I laugh. "With respect, obviously."

"The key to any successful relationship," he shoots back.

"Is that what this is?" I ask, before I can think better of it. The fluorescent lights overhead feel unforgivingly bright all of a sudden. "A relationship?"

Gray raises his eyebrows. "You tell me."

I bite my lip. On one hand, I'd be lying if I said I didn't feel something for him, that being with him doesn't light a spark inside me, doesn't fill my heart like a balloon inside my chest. On the other hand . . .

"I don't think you're a lot," I tell him finally, which isn't really an answer to his question. "Or I mean, okay, you can be. A lot, I mean. But in a good way." I reach for his hand, the calluses on his palm scraping gently against my skin. "I would never tell you to fuck off. I mean, I'd never tell any-one to fuck off, let's be real. But especially not you."

Gray smiles. "Too polite, huh?"

"Something like that," I tell him.

"Well," he says, "you never know. You might surprise yourself. Maybe one of these days you'll snap and start tell-ing people to fuck themselves left and right."

"Maybe." I hold up the doughnut bag. "Peace offer-ing?"

"There better be bear claws in there," he says, and kisses me before I can reply.

TWENTY-SIX

I'm in the bathroom near the gym on Friday morning when the door to the stall beside me opens and Chloe comes out.

"Oh! Sorry," I say, motioning at the sinks; there are only two in this bathroom, and only one of them has any water pressure. "Go ahead."

Chloe shakes her head, blond hair bouncing; today the lapel pin on her uniform collar is shaped like a tiny palm tree. "No," she says, "you can go."

"No, really."

"Marin," Chloe says, an impatient edge creeping into her voice. "Just go, okay?"

"Okay. Sorry." I wash my hands as fast as humanly possible, wrinkling my nose at the smell of the cheap green soap and grabbing a paper towel from the dispenser.

"So, um," I try, sensing an opening. "How's your day going?"

As an opening gambit it's pretty pathetic; Chloe's expression makes that much abundantly clear.

"It's fine. No complaints."

"That's good." I pull the sleeves of my uniform sweater down over my hands, wanting to howl at the thought of things being this awkward and impossible between us forever. *It's just me*, I want to tell her. *I'm still the same person I was before.*

"Look," I tell her, "I know this is a long shot, but there's a book club potluck tonight, if you're interested."

Chloe blinks at me. "A potluck?" she repeats.

"I know," I say, suddenly embarrassed by the earnestness of it—it's the kind of thing we probably would have made fun of, three months ago. "It's kind of like, very Midwestern mom of us? But it could be fun, right? And you don't have to be in the book club to come, so . . ."

Chloe nods slowly. "Um, thanks," she says. "I've got other plans, but . . . sounds fun."

I wince. *Other plans*, like she's some vague acquaintance

on the T who doesn't want to come to my weird church group and not the person who knows me best and longest, who always comes into a one-person bathroom with me when we're out together and whose house I've thrown up in on two separate occasions.

"Sure thing," I tell her. "Maybe another time, then."

"Maybe," Chloe says, leaning over the sink to reapply her lipstick. Neither one of us says goodbye before I go.

After Gray's practice, we head over to the potluck together, his heavy hand on mine. I've always kind of liked being in school when it's dark out, how it feels weirdly festive; Lydia and Elisa made decorations for the bio lab, brightly colored paper bunting hung up above the whiteboard, and a bunch of desks are pushed together and draped with a purple plastic cloth. Gray brought brownies one of his moms made, studded with walnuts and caramel chips and topped with flaky sea salt. Dave stopped at McDonald's and got like five dozen Chicken McNuggets, and Chloe's dad sent me with a huge to-go container of lamb meatballs with a yogurt dipping sauce from the restaurant. Even Ms. Klein brought something, though she's always talking about how she doesn't ever turn her oven on—tiny crostini spread with herby cheese and dolloped with fancy blackberry jam.

This is the first time we've all hung out where we didn't have a specific book to talk about, and I was worried it might be as awkward as it was back at the very beginning, but to my surprise the room is echoing with conversations: Bri and Maddie, the jazz band freshmen who've been showing up since the very beginning, are debating whether cheerleading is inherently sexist, while Dave and Gray scroll through Gray's phone, putting together a playlist of pump-up jams.

"My boyfriend is obsessed with this one," Dave says, hitting play on what I think is the new Halsey. He dates a super cute guy on the track team who's dropped in on a couple of our meetings and knew a surprising amount about feminist film theory.

"It's also important to think about the ways that women of color are left out of the conversation," Ms. Klein is saying when I drift over toward the dessert table. "Like when people say that women make seventy-seven cents on the dollar, what they mean is white women. For black women it's sixty-three cents on the dollar. And for Latina women it's even less."

"It's fifty-four cents," Elisa pipes up from across the room, then goes back to talking with Fiona Tyler, a sophomore who joined the club a couple of weeks ago, about some musical show on the CW they both like.

"No offense," Lydia says, crossing her ankles and leaning back on the desk she's perched on, "but when it comes to feminism, or whatever, it feels like white ladies always kind of want to make the conversation about them. Like they're the only ones whose ideas or priorities anyone should listen to."

My first reaction is to feel defensive—that's not what I'm doing, is it?—but then I take a breath, thinking about everything I thought I knew about feminism before I started the book club. I know that I've still got a ton left to learn.

"I can see that," I admit. "Like I remember reading an article about the original name of the Women's March being a rip-off of the Million Man March, and when black activists pointed that out a bunch of white women got all offended."

"Yeah, that's one example," Lydia says, though from her expression I can tell it's nowhere near the most important one. "But basically it's just that a lot of white women have this idea that feminism can be separated out from race or sexual identity or ability or any of that—and it can't. If you're going to go in, you have to go all in, you know?"

"The Audre Lorde essay we're going to be talking about next week is a great example of how different identities and marginalizations intersect and inform each other," Ms. Klein says, nibbling the corner of a brownie. "And you guys put *Her Body and Other Parties* on the list of books you might want to tackle, right?"

"That book is awesome," Gray says immediately. "And, like, super gory."

I look at him in surprise. "You've read it?"

He shrugs. "My mom got it for me, 'cause I said I liked Stephen King."

The conversation wanders from there—from *Pet Sematary* to who bought winter formal tickets and who they're taking, to the new werewolf show that just went up on Netflix, to a short biography of Ida B. Wells that Fiona pulls up on her phone when Dave admits to not knowing who she is. She's just finishing up when I notice Gray sneaking a look at his messages.

"You got another date?" I ask, nudging him gently in the side.

He shakes his head. "There's a party at Hurley Dubcek's," he admits. "I was going to ask you if you wanted to go after this, but I didn't want you to think I didn't want to be here." Gray looks around. "Because I do," he says resolutely, like he thinks he's running for political office. "Want to be here."

"Okay, big feminist," I say, patting him reassuringly on the shoulder. "We believe you."

"I was going to swing by that party too, actually," Lydia pipes up. "If anybody wants a ride."

There's a moment of awkward quiet then, all of us looking around at each other, none of us wanting to be the first to bail.

Finally Ms. Klein lets out a snort. "Get out of here," she says, popping one last meatball into her mouth before snapping the lid back onto the take-out container. "Make good choices, et cetera. I'll see you guys next week."

TWENTY-SEVEN

Hurley Dubcek lives in one of those quintessential Massachusetts houses that's been around since the colonies, with a steeply pitched roof and no real front porch, like maybe they didn't have time for things like that back then because there was too much butter to be churned. As we walk past an antique china cabinet in the narrow hallway all the delicate-looking dishes rattle ominously.

"I always feel like a frickin' monster in places like this," Gray murmurs over my shoulder.

I nod. "I was just thinking that exact same thing about you."

He looks at me, mock horror on his handsome face. "Rude!"

I grin at him. "I'm kidding." I reach back and take his hand, lacing our fingers together and squeezing once before releasing him. "Come on."

We pull a couple of warm cans from a thirty-pack in the kitchen, watching as Elisa grabs Lydia a Diet Coke from the fridge before pulling Dave in the direction of the backyard. Gray lets out a low whistle.

"Check out book club," he says with a smile. In the end almost everyone who was at the potluck wound up coming, all of us rolling down the windows in Lydia's mom's van and singing along to the radio at the tops of our lungs. "Ready to rage."

"I was surprised they all showed up tonight," I admit as we edge through the crowd into the living room, where someone has pushed aside what looks like a hundred-year-old leather sofa to make room to dance on the knotty wood floors. "To the potluck, I mean. Honestly, I'm surprised they show up at the actual meetings too, but you know what I'm saying."

"Kind of." Gray shrugs, tilting his head back against the wall in between two ancient-looking botanical prints. "They're showing up because of you though."

I laugh. "Maybe *you* are."

"I'm serious," Gray counters with a frown. "It's not just me. It's cool, what you started."

"Well," I say, suddenly self-conscious. I look out in the living room, where Dean Shepherd is attempting an extremely rudimentary pop-and-lock situation near the enormous stone fireplace. "Thanks."

"Don't mention it." Gray lifts his chin. "You want to dance?"

I raise my eyebrows. "Do *you*?"

"Always." He takes my hand, pulling me into the living room. "Come on."

Gray is the most enthusiastic dancer I've ever met, which in no way means he's good at it—arms and legs everywhere, a goofy, uncoordinated shuffle. I wonder what it's like not to care about what people think—although, yes, it's certainly easier not to care what people think when you're a six-foot-tall lacrosse star with a reputation for getting a million girls.

Just for tonight though, I don't want to worry about that. I close my eyes and shake my hair and let Gray twirl me around—liking the winter-woods smell of him, the feeling of his chest pressed against my back.

Eventually Dave comes and rounds us up for a game of book club beer pong; I promise to meet them outside before detouring toward the powder room tucked underneath the staircase in the front hall. I twist the creaky glass knob, pulling the door open—and almost trip right over Chloe, who's sitting with her knees pulled up on the tile. "Whoops," I say, holding up my hands to show I come in peace. "Sorry."

"It's fine," Chloe mumbles, tipping her head back against the peeling toile-patterned wallpaper. Her eyeliner is migrating down her face. "I was just leaving."

She curls her fingers around the sink, pulling herself unsteadily to her feet. "I—whoops." She stumbles a little, bracing her free hand against the wall.

I frown. So this was what she meant by "other plans." I haven't seen her this drunk since fall of freshman year, when we experimented with the peach schnapps at the back of my parents' liquor cabinet and wound up throwing up all over my basement by 9:00 p.m.

"Are you okay?" I can't help asking.

"I'm fine," she snaps, then immediately turns and barfs up a stomach full of bright blue party punch. She makes the toilet, thank God, but just barely; I reach over and gather her hair back like an instinct, just like she did for me last year when I puked in the bushes behind her house after spring formal. Both of us can just barely fit in here at once.

When she's finally finished I pass her a wad of TP to wipe her mouth with, tucking my hands in my pockets and looking discreetly away as she pulls herself together.

"Um," she says, clearing her throat and swiping her thumbs under her eyes to wipe the makeup away. "Thanks."

"No problem," I say, with the kind of polite *Don't worry about it* smile you offer someone when they've only got one item at the grocery store and you're letting them cut ahead of you in line. "You got a ride home?"

I'm prepared for some variation of *You're not my fucking mother*, but instead Chloe just nods.

"Emily is going to take me," she says, and I nod back.

"That's good." We stand there for a moment, looking at each other. This is *Chloe*, I remind myself, who taught me how to do an understated cat eye and is allergic to apples unless you microwave them for ten seconds first and can recite the entire second season of *Parks and Rec* from memory. I know her like I know Gracie; I know her like I know myself. But it feels like I'm looking at a stranger.

"Okay," I say finally. "Well. Have a good night, then."

"You too," Chloe says. She looks at me for a long moment, her eyes suddenly clear and focused. "Listen, Marin—" she starts, then abruptly breaks off. "Never mind," she says, and it's like I can see the moment she changes her mind about saying whatever it is she's got to say to me. "I'll see you."

"No, hey, wait." I've been edging out of the tiny bathroom, but suddenly I stop. "What's up?"

Chloe shakes her head. "It's nothing," she says, curling her fingers around the doorjamb for balance and brushing past me. "I'll see you around."

So . . . That's that, I guess.

I pee and wash my hands and make my way out into the backyard, which boasts a statue of a gnome holding a gazing ball, a tiny wishing well complete with crank and wooden bucket, and one of those little decorative ponds you can fill with Japanese koi. In this case it seems to be mostly filled with muck, which isn't stopping a bunch of people from playing catch across the diameter of it, one of those old Nerf footballs with the fin on the back of it sailing through the air. Gray and the rest of the book club are still negotiating the rules of this alleged beer pong tournament, though suddenly the last thing I want to do is play some dumb drinking game.

"I'm not having fun anymore," I announce, and Gray frowns.

"Can't have that," he says. Then, more seriously: "Everything okay?"

"Yeah." I offer him a smile; I want to explain about Chloe, but I don't want to do it here. "You want to maybe bail though?"

There's a part of me that's expecting him to be kind of a dick about it, but instead Gray just nods right away, taking my hand as we turn to go. That's when I hear a scoff off to my left, and when I turn I see Jacob. A bottle of Coors dangles from his fingers.

"Can I help you?" I ask.

"Just enjoying this little lovefest," he calls from the edge of the mucky pond. He's even drunker than Chloe, if that's possible. There's a mean, hard glint in his eye. He turns to Gray, his nasty smirk morphing into a faux-magnanimous smile.

"It's cool if you want my sloppy seconds, dude," he says, slurring just a little. "And Bex's too, I guess."

I take an instinctive step back, shocked as if he'd slapped me. There's a moment when I feel, horribly, like I'm about to cry.

"What did you just say?" Gray asks. His voice is perfectly pleasant—friendly, even—but he lets go of my hand as he takes a step closer to Jacob, who squares his shoulders and holds his ground.

"You heard me," he says, lifting his arrogant chin.

Gray nods easily. "I did," he agrees, taking a step closer, then another; now Jacob *does* back up, only he's misjudged how close he is to the side of the algae-covered pond. A slippery rock gives way under his foot and he goes pinwheeling backward, landing in the chilly, smelly water with a splash so noisy and dramatic half the party breaks into applause.

Gray looks at Jacob for a moment, then back at me, trying not to laugh and doing an overall admirable job of it.

"Sorry," he says, sounding a little sheepish. "I know you don't need me to protect you."

I reach to cup his face with both hands, stamping a kiss on his mouth like a seal of approval. "You know," I say, "I think I can make an exception just this once."

I don't have to be home for an hour yet, so we swing by Gray's house, a tidy Cape Cod with carefully tarped rosebushes planted underneath the windows and a porch light shaped like a star hanging over the red front door. Inside it's warm, the air fragrant with the scent of sandalwood incense; I spy the orange flash of a cat as she darts up the stairs.

"Home!" Gray calls, hanging our coats on a hook by the doorway.

"In here!" a woman's voice calls back.

Gray leads me through the living room, which is lined

with bookshelves on two walls and art prints on the others, a blue velvet couch facing a pair of architectural-looking chairs. It's not how I pictured his house, and it must show on my face, because Gray nudges me in the side. "Were you imagining like, the whole place decorated in the colors of the New England Patriots?" he asks.

"Shut up," I say, though he's definitely on to me at this point. "No."

"You totally were," he says with a laugh, then nods at the bookshelves. "How exactly did you think I came up with a copy of *The Handmaid's Tale* so fast?"

He leads me through the formal living room and into a den, where two women are sitting watching *Brooklyn Nine-Nine* and drinking wine, a second orange cat purring on the sofa between them.

"Hey, baby," one of them says, lifting her face so that Gray can drop a kiss onto her cheek.

"This is Marin," he says. "These are my moms, Heather and Jenn."

"*This* is Marin!" the brunette—Jenn, I think—crows, like she's heard about me before.

I smile.

"Mom," Gray says, looking faintly embarrassed. "Jesus."

215

We chat for a little while, about the book club and about my editorials for the *Beacon*, which I guess he also mentioned.

"How was the party?" Heather asks.

"Kind of boring," Gray says, though I'm not entirely sure if he means the potluck or Hurley's; either way, he leaves out the part about Jacob and the algae pond. "We're gonna get some food and go upstairs."

"Door open!" Heather calls after us, and Gray makes a face for my benefit.

"Noted!" he calls back. Then, more quietly, "Jesus *Christ*, Mom."

"We heard that!" Heather yells.

We head into the kitchen, which looks like it was recently redone, with stainless appliances and a big window above the sink overlooking the yard.

"Can I ask you something?" I say, hopping up onto a stool. "Do you call both your moms 'Mom'?"

That makes him smile. "I mean, yeah," he says, opening a box of Cheez-Its and digging out a bright orange handful. "What else would I call them?"

"No, I just mean, how do you keep them straight?"

Gray gives me a weird look, like possibly he's never stopped to think about it before. "Well, I mean, there's only two of them," he points out. "And my sister always just kind of . . . knows which one I'm talking about? I don't know. I didn't think it was weird until right this minute, so thanks for that, I guess."

"You're welcome," I say with a smile, taking the box of crackers from his outstretched hand. "Also, I gotta say— obviously I don't know them, but those guys don't seem like the type to get super worked up over whether you play lacrosse in college."

Gray's eyes narrow. "In the five minutes you talked to them?" he asks pointedly, and I can tell I've hit a nerve.

"Okay, fine," I say, "Fair enough."

"They just . . . want me to be a college guy, that's all." Gray shrugs. "And if I can't get in on my grades, then . . ." He trails off. "I don't know," he says, picking the box of Cheez-Its up off the counter and using it to usher me out of the kitchen. "I'll figure it out."

"You will," I promise, and follow him up the stairs.

Gray's room is less of a surprise than the rest of the house, with white walls and bluish carpet and a signed Tom Brady jersey hanging in a poster frame above the desk. The bed is unmade, with rumpled flannel sheets melting off the edge of it. Gray scoops a pair of boxers off the floor and chucks them into the closet, looking goofily embarrassed.

"Sorry," he says. "If I knew you were coming—" He breaks off, seeming to think about it for a moment. "Well, no, honestly. I probably still would have been a total slob."

"Monster," I tease, glancing around the room at the half-empty water glasses clustered on every available surface, paperbacks for book club stacked haphazardly on the desk. On the dresser is a photo of his moms standing on either side of a little boy with a slightly uneven bowl cut, his front teeth bucked like a cartoon character's.

"Oh my gosh," I say, reaching for it before I can stop myself. "Is this you?"

"Nah," Gray says immediately, "it's just some other little kid I keep pictures of in my bedroom."

"Shut up," I tell him, completely unable to keep the grin off my face. "You were cute."

"I was . . . desperately in need of a haircut and twelve thousand dollars' worth of orthodontia," Gray counters, sitting down on the edge of the bed and leaning back on his palms. "That picture keeps me humble."

"Oh, right," I say seriously, crossing the carpet to stand between his knees, his shoulders warm and broad and solid underneath my hands. "Because otherwise your ego would just explode all over the place, huh?"

"Oh, totally out of control," Gray confirms with a smile.

"I mean, what with my athletic achievements, my outstanding academic record—"

"Your legendary prowess with the ladies," I put in.

"I'm also tall," he says, curling his fingers around my waist and pulling me closer. "Don't forget about that."

"I would never," I murmur, wrapping my arms around his neck and angling my face down until he gets the message and kisses me. I breathe a tiny sigh against his mouth. We've done this enough over the last few weeks that it's starting to feel normal, which isn't to say the thrill of it has worn off—the opposite, actually. Kissing Gray isn't like anything else I've ever done. It's not that I never enjoyed myself, fooling around with Jacob, but the truth is I never totally got what the big deal was. Half the time in my head I'd be somewhere else entirely—worrying over a missed problem on that morning's calc test, replaying an argument with my mom—and I don't think he ever actually noticed.

With Gray I feel achingly, deliciously alert.

Eventually he eases us back onto the mattress, the smell of detergent and sleep and boy all around me. The door is still open, but his room is far enough from the top of the stairs that the effect is the same as if we were the only ones in the house. Gray's fingertips creep up under the hem of my T-shirt, touching the sensitive skin of my waist and tracing the very bottom of my rib cage. I shiver, and Gray's eyes fly open.

"This okay?" he asks, gaze searching.

I pull back and look at him for a moment, hit by that sudden zing of recognition I never felt before.

I see you, I want to tell him. *I think you see me too.* "Yeah," I tell him. "This is good."

TWENTY-EIGHT

Gray's got a lacrosse game the following Thursday, so I head off to book club without him—we read "Age, Race, Class and Sex," this week, and I was thinking about suggesting we watch the PBS documentary about Audre Lorde, but when I walk into Ms. Klein's classroom after eighth period Dave looks surprised to see me at all.

"You're here?" he asks, pulling a bag of pretzels and a tub of onion dip out of his backpack. It was his turn to bring snacks today. "Doesn't Gray have that big game against Hartley?"

"I mean, yeah," I say, ignoring the twinge of guilt I feel

at missing it—the same twinge I've been feeling all day, truth be told. "But he gets it."

"Really?" Elisa puts in, dropping her shoulder bag on the floor and plunking down in an empty seat next to Ms. Klein. "That's the school he got kicked out of, isn't it? Feels like kind of a big deal."

"Thanks a lot," I say, snagging a couple of pretzels out of the bag and crunching thoughtfully. "I don't know. I guess I didn't want to be that girl, you know? The one who drops her commitments to go cheer on some dude."

"I don't think there's anything wrong with supporting somebody you care about," Elisa says, holding her hand out for the pretzel bag and waggling her long fingers until I pass it over. "I mean, you guys all came to my game, didn't you?"

"I mean, sure," I say, "but that's different."

"Why, because she's a girl?" Dave asks. "Isn't that reverse sexism?"

"Reverse sexism is one hundred percent not a thing," Lydia says immediately.

"Well, let's dig into that," Ms. Klein says, setting her book of essays down on the desk like she suddenly suspects we won't be getting to it any time soon. "Can anyone explain to me *why* it's not a thing?"

"Because men unequivocally have more power than

women in our society," Maddie says easily, and I look at her in surprise—she's been pretty quiet at meetings up until now, but her voice is confident and clear. "It's like how racism against white people isn't a thing."

Ms. Klein nods. "Racism—and sexism, and ableism—are all power structures," she explains. "They're systems of oppression that are larger than any one interaction. So when we're thinking about them, it's important for us to ask ourselves what groups of people have historically been in charge in our society, and how the ways that our institutions are set up make it possible for those same groups to hold on to that power."

"So, just to throw out a random, totally hypothetical example," Elisa says pointedly, "a system where the entire school dress code is way more restrictive for girls than it is for guys—that would be sexism. Whereas Marin not going to Gray's game because she's trying to prove some point about something—"

"That's just dumb," Lydia finishes triumphantly.

"Hey!" I protest, but I'm laughing. After all, it's not like they're wrong. As much as I love this book club, I can't act like I don't wish I was somewhere other than here today. I care about Gray, as much as I've tried to keep myself from admitting it. I want to be there to cheer him on.

Elisa glances at the clock about the doorway. "Game doesn't start till four, right?" she asks, raising her eyebrows. "I propose a field trip."

"All in favor?" Dave asks, and a half-dozen hands go up around the classroom.

I feel myself grin.

Hartley is only about twenty minutes away, the bleachers packed with onlookers and the whole place smelling faintly of locker room. Ms. Klein tagged along too in the end, following us in her tidy little Volkswagen, and the group of us find spots on the Bridgewater side, the fluorescent lights casting everyone's face slightly green.

"There's Gray!" says Maddie, throwing a hand up to wave as we get ourselves settled near the top of the bleachers. I duck my face to hide my own instinctive eye roll at how swoony she sounds, but when I look up again Gray's gazing right at me, and just like that the expression on his face erases any weirdness I felt about coming here. He looks—there is no other way to describe this, or the way it sets something burning warmly in my chest—*delighted*.

Even after dating Jacob for the better part of a year, I have no idea what the rules of lacrosse are, honestly, but I like watching Gray running around down there—the easy way his body moves inside his red-and-gold uniform, the concentration on his handsome face. I know he's got mixed feelings about playing for St. Lawrence next year, but it's obvious he could if he wanted to: he's a natural leader, shouting casual encouragement at his teammates even as he bolts down the length of the gym.

Our team's leading 3–2 and Gray's heading for another goal when one of the guys from Hartley juts his lacrosse stick out in what looks to me like a purposeful jab. Gray spots it and tries to sidestep, but he's not quite fast enough, and all at once he trips and hits the floor with a thud I feel in my spine. Beside me, Ms. Klein gasps, the kind of sound you never really want to hear from an authority figure. Lydia lets out a low, quiet swear.

For a moment Gray lies still, unmoving; the ref blows his whistle, and a murmur goes up in the stands. Before I even know I'm going to do it I'm out of my seat and scrambling down the bleachers, darting through the crowd and out onto the field.

"You can't be out here!" one of the refs calls to me, but I'm not listening. Normally this is never something I would do—purposely drawing attention to myself, making a scene—but lately I've been realizing exactly what I *will* do, with a good enough reason.

And Gray is a good enough reason.

He's struggling to sit up as I reach him, another ref and Coach Arwen and a bunch of guys from the team circled around him in concern. His ankle is already starting to swell.

"I'm calling an ambulance," Coach is saying, digging his cell phone out of his pocket.

"No, no, no, I definitely don't need that," Gray protests, but when he tries to get to his feet his whole face goes sweaty and ghost pale.

"Okay," he says, sitting back down hard on the floor with a grimace. "Maybe I do."

He seems to register me for the first time then. "Hi," he says.

"Hi," I say. "You want me to call your moms?"

Gray shakes his head. "You can, but it's going to be hard to get them," he tells me. "My mom's got a late-afternoon class. And my mom's in court." He looks at me, offering a weak smile; he's hurting badly, that much is clear, though he's trying not to show it.

"See, this would be one of those times where it would be useful for me to call them two different things."

The ambulance arrives a few minutes later, a pair of tersely efficient paramedics peppering Gray with questions, moving his ankle gently this way and that. The one who's a woman doesn't look much older than us.

Do you know what you're doing? I want to ask her, flinching as Gray grimaces in obvious discomfort. *Do you know how important he is?*

Finally they seem to agree it's likely broken and he needs to get an X-ray, boosting him to his good foot and loading him up onto a stretcher. He's taller than both of them, and broader; they remind me of a couple in a fairy tale trying to transport a fallen giant.

"I'll get over there as soon as I can," Coach Arwen tells Gray, taking off his hat and scrubbing a nervous hand through his salt-and-pepper hair so it sticks up in all directions like the scientist from *Back to the Future*. "Do you want to have one of the guys ride along with you, keep you company?"

"I'll go," I hear myself say.

The crowd of faces turn to look at me at once. "Who are you?" the male EMT asks.

"I'm his girlfriend," I blurt.

Gray raises his eyebrows with a smile. This is the first time I've used the g-word in front of him. Actually, it's the first time I've used it at all.

I leave messages for both his moms on our way to the

227

hospital, then settle myself in a waiting room chair while the nurse takes him for X-rays, texting my own parents and the rest of the book club to let them know what's going on.

Tell Gray we love him! Elisa texts back, along with a string of on-theme emojis. *We won the game.*

Finally the nurses let me go and hang out with him while we wait for the X-rays to come back.

"Hi," I say, sitting down in the visitor's chair beside his hospital bed. He's still in his lacrosse uniform, a stretch of painful-looking turf burn on his forearm from where he fell.

"I'm on a lot of drugs," Gray announces grandly. "So, you know. No funny business."

"I would never," I assure him, looking down at my hands for a moment. Lately I've been biting my fingernails again, a habit I kicked back in second grade when my mom took to painting them with white vinegar, and my cuticles are ragged and raw.

Gray smiles a lazy, loopy smile. "It was nice hearing you call yourself my girlfriend back there."

I grin and roll my eyes. "It seemed faster than identifying myself as, like, founder of your feminist book club and new pal who sometimes hangs out in your bedroom."

He leans his head back against the pillow, his gaze surprisingly keen. "It does have kind of a ring to it, I guess.

Then again, so does girlfriend." He reaches for my hand. "I like you so, so much, Marin," he tells me. "And not just because I'm a little stoned at this particular moment, and not just because I can't get enough feminist theory in my life. I think you're smart. I think you're funny. And I think you're fierce as all hell."

I try to stave off the sudden rush of emotion—fear of getting hurt again, relief that he's okay, and something altogether bigger and warmer than that, something that fills my chest until it feels like I might burst from the sheer expansive size of it. "I bet you say that to all the girls," I finally say.

I'm kidding, but Gray doesn't smile.

"I don't, actually," he says as he sits up in his hospital bed. "I really don't." He tugs on my hand then, pulling me forward until our faces are nearly touching.

"You my girlfriend?" he asks, and his voice is so quiet.

I'm too busy kissing him to reply.

TWENTY-NINE

Second-semester seniors are allowed to leave campus during their free periods, so on Tuesday I run out to Panera for bagels and lattes, then come back and meet Gray in the common area outside the library, where he's reading *A Room of One's Own* for book club with his busted ankle propped up on a bench. It's just a bad sprain, but he's on crutches for a couple of weeks at least.

"Eh," he said when the doctor told him, "only a couple of games left anyway."

I couldn't help but notice he didn't sound all that broken up about it. He still hasn't talked to his moms about college.

"My hero," he says now, taking his bagel and lifting his face to kiss me before holding the book up for my inspection.

"This one's super fucking boring," he reports.

"Oh, shush," I chide, though the truth is I read the first fifty pages last night and it's not like he's wrong, exactly. I sit down on the bench beside him, taking a sip of my latte before reaching into my backpack and clicking the mail icon on my phone. If Mr. DioGuardi catches you even looking at your phone during school hours he'll take it for the rest of the day, where it sits in a big basket in the admin suite labeled with a picture of an anthropomorphic iPhone crying enormous cartoon tears that he must have printed off the internet, but Brown notifications are going out this week, and I've been refreshing my email every fifteen minutes. I checked while I waited at Panera, and then again before I came back into school, but this time when I click over I can't hold back a quiet gasp: there's BROWN UNIVERSITY OFFICE OF ADMISSIONS in the sender line.

Gray looks up from his book. "Hm?"

I shake my head instead of answering. When I pictured this moment—and let's be real, I've been picturing this moment more or less since freshman year—I was always sitting calmly at home on my laptop, a mug of tea beside me and a cat curled in my lap, the hugeness and inevitability of the occasion somehow managing to overcome the inconvenience of the facts that I don't drink tea or have a cat. Now I force myself to take a breath, to take in the scene around me—the crispy January grass out the window, the faintly medicinal smell of Gray's face wash, the crinkly brown Panera bag in my lap. I want to remember exactly how this feels.

Dear Marin,
Thank you for your interest in Brown University.
Unfortunately, I'm very sorry to inform you that we
are unable to offer you admission for the upcoming
academic year.

I feel the blood drain out of my face, pins and needles prickling in the tips of my fingers. For a long, disorienting moment, I can't get the words to compute.

I didn't get in.

I didn't even make the *wait* list.

The letter goes on from there, explaining how many applications they receive and how rigorous the admission process is, reassuring me that just because I didn't get into Brown doesn't mean I don't have a bright academic future ahead of me, but it's like the whole thing is written in a language I don't understand. My heart slams against my rib cage. My hands and feet are cold and numb. This is just one more situation I totally misjudged, I realize grimly: I was overconfident, too sure I was in control of what was happening. I played it all wrong.

Gray glances over at me again, a tiny divot appearing between his thick, straight eyebrows. "Everything okay?" he asks.

"Um," I say, swallowing down a lump the size of a pair of gym socks stuck at the back of my throat. "Yup." I can't bring myself to tell him, and as soon as I have that thought I remember that somehow I'm going to have to tell my parents—God, that I'm going to have to tell *Gram* when it's all she's ever wanted for me—and that's when I start to feel like I might throw up.

I thought I was a shoo-in. How could I have been so dumb?

Wait a minute, I think, my head clearing briefly. I thought I was a shoo-in because my interviewer essentially told me I was.

"Um," I say, getting to my feet so quickly the paper bag slides to the tile; I bend down and scoop it up before thrusting it in Gray's direction, swinging my still-open backpack onto one shoulder. "I just remembered I left my notes for next period in the car. I'll see you at lunch, okay?"

"Uh, yeah." Gray's eyes narrow a little. "Sure."

Then, laying one big hand on my arm: "Marin," he says, "Are you sure you're okay? You just got, like, super weird all of a sudden."

"Yup," I call over my shoulder, pulling gently away and darting down the hallway toward the exit. "Everything's fine!"

Out in the parking lot I dig wildly through my backpack until I find the business card Kalina gave me on the day of the interview; it's crumpled at the bottom, crumb-stained and soft around the edges. I dial her office number with shaking hands, squinting up at the midmorning sunlight.

"Marin," Kalina says, once the front desk assistant puts me through to her office. Right away she sounds uncomfortable, and I wonder if any authority figure is ever going to be happy to hear from me again. "How are you?"

"Um, not great, actually." I dig the nails of my free hand into my palm, trying not to sound hysterical. I've only got six more minutes until I have to be in class. "I just got a rejection letter from your office."

Kalina makes a sympathetic sound. "Oof, I'm sorry to hear that," she says. "You know, the university gets over thirty thousand applicants each year, and there's such a limited number of spots that often even when a candidate is qualified—"

"No, I know," I interrupt. "It says so in the letter. And I'm sorry if it's inappropriate to be calling you like this. I know it's probably bad form. But I just wanted to know what happened. For, like, the future."

"Unfortunately I can't really speak to the specifics," Kalina says. "We've got a policy of not commenting on individual applicants—again, the pool is just so large—"

"Kalina," I say, and my voice is dangerously close to be breaking. "Please? You had all the information when we met, right? And you said—"

"I shouldn't have," she interrupts me. "I know you and I had a rapport, but I was speaking out of turn, and I'm sorry if I—"

"Was it my grades?" I ask. "My extracurriculars? What?"

Kalina doesn't say anything for a moment. It's like I can feel her debating something with herself on the other end of the line. "Look, Marin," she says, and her voice is very quiet. "Ultimately the admissions board received some information that made us feel like you might be a better fit elsewhere, that's all."

All at once I stand up a little straighter, a sensation like a spider scuttling up along my spine. "What information?"

"Marin, I really can't—"

"What information? Kalina, if somebody said something about me that made it so I can't get into *college*—" I shake my head, catching a glimpse of the window of the newspaper office out of the very corner of my eye; then, all at once, the penny drops. "Oh my god. Was it Bex?"

"I'm sorry?"

"Mr. Beckett," I say. "Jon Beckett, my English teacher. He—he and I—his family are these huge donors, and—" I break off. "Is that who it was?"

For a long time Kalina doesn't answer, and that's how I know that it's true.

"For what it's worth, I went to bat for you," she tells me finally. "I'm really sorry it didn't work out."

"Yeah," I say, dimly aware of the bell for the end of the period ringing in the distance. I tilt my head back and look up at the tree line, my eyes blurring with tears. "Me too."

THIRTY

I stumble back into the building, my chest tight and my breath coming in frantic, ragged gulps. I feel like I could rip tree trunks in half with my bare hands or burst into flames in the middle of the hallway. In the back of my mind I know that not getting into my first-choice Ivy League university is the very definition of a champagne problem: after all, there are plenty of other colleges. There are plenty of other paths.

But this is the one I wanted. This is the one I *earned*.

And he just . . . took it.

There's only one concrete thought in my head as I careen down the hallway:

I have to find him.

I know from back when we used to be friends, or whatever it is I thought we were, that Bex doesn't have a class this period. I head for the newspaper office, but the room is dark and empty when I arrive, the Bridgewater screensavers glowing vacantly on the computer screens.

I try the cafeteria next, then the admin suite where the copier is, coming up empty. I'm fully prepared to march right into the teachers' lounge, to interrupt whatever secret, sacred stuff they all do in there with their microwave and their electric kettle, but instead, when I turn the corner near Ms. Klein's lab there he is strolling down the hallway in my direction, his stupid messenger bag slung across his chest.

I gasp, freezing for one icy moment before I manage to make any words. "Um," I announce, the sound coming out phlegmy and garbled. "I need to talk to you."

Bex frowns. "Marin," he says, with this tiny pause like I'm some random student he's never taught before and he needs to search his mental contacts list for my name. "Shouldn't you be in class?"

"I don't think it really matters at this point, does it?" I shoot back. "You made sure of that."

Bex's eyes narrow for the briefest of moments. "Well, it's pretty obvious you're upset," he observes mildly, like the emotion has nothing whatsoever to do with him, like I'm a character on a TV show he doesn't much like. "Do you want to go somewhere and talk?"

"Somewhere like your apartment, you mean?"

It's out before I can stop myself, and I think I shock us both in equal part: Bex's lips thin, a muscle twitching erratically in his jaw.

"This is really inappropriate," he murmurs with a shake of his head, turning away and making to brush past me down the hallway. "If you want to have a conversation related to your schoolwork, you know where to—"

I laugh out loud, hysterical and cackling like the witches from *Macbeth*. I know I sound exactly as crazy and ungovernable as everyone in this school already thinks I am, but for the first time since this all started I 100 percent do not care.

"Seriously?" I can't help asking. "*I'm* inappropriate?"

"*Enough*." All at once Bex turns around again, grabbing me by the arm and steering me down the hallway into the south stairwell, the door slamming shut behind us with a startling *chunk*. "Jesus *Christ*, Marin," he says, bewildered. "What is your problem right now?"

In the back of my head it occurs to me to be afraid of him. Instead, I stand my ground, planting my feet on the linoleum and willing my voice not to shake. "Did you talk to the Brown admissions board about me?"

Bex's expression doesn't change, smooth and innocent as a Boy Scout's, but his hands twitch at his sides.

"I— What makes you think that?" he asks, and then he clears his throat, and that's when I know I've got him.

"You did." Even after everything that's happened there's a part of me that didn't believe it until right this moment, like surely no adult—no *teacher*—could be that awful and petty and mean. "Oh my god."

"First of all—"

"How could you do this to me?" I interrupt, trying like all hell to swallow the sob I feel rising in my throat. Sounding a little emotional is one thing. Letting him see me cry is quite another. "Brown has been my dream my entire freaking life."

Bex lets out a low, mean scoff. "I ruined your *dream*?" he echoes contemptuously, like I'm a little kid who still believes in Santa Claus. "You tried to ruin my *life*, Marin."

For a moment I'm totally stunned. "I—what?"

Bex rolls his eyes, scrubbing a hand through his hair like he honestly cannot believe me. "My god," he says, "you are so spoiled. Everyone in this school is spoiled, but especially you."

I blink at him for a moment, caught up short. No adult has ever talked to me that way before. "How am I spoiled?" I ask, more baffled than offended. "You're the one who—"

"You can play victim all you want, kiddo," Bex interrupts. "You can act like you had nothing to do with any of this. But you and I both know the truth."

I feel myself get very still. "What does that mean?"

"Oh, don't look at me like that. You're not a baby deer." Bex rolls his eyes. "You were always around, Marin. Hanging out in the office. Making up excuses to ask for rides."

"Wait a second," I protest. "I never—"

"Sitting on my fucking desk, for Christ's sake," Bex continues. "What vibe did you think you were giving off, exactly? You wanted it, Marin. And maybe you freaked out and regretted it afterward, but I'm not going to sit around and let you make me out to be some kind of fucking sex predator when we both know you were every bit as responsible for what happened as I was. More, probably."

I am crying now, I can't even help it, tears slipping fast and silent down my face. For the first time in my life it's like I'm all out of words.

"Fuck you," is all I can manage. I don't wait for him to reply before I turn and walk away.

THIRTY-ONE

I tear down the hallway toward the south exit, slamming the push bar and exploding out into the parking lot even though it's the middle of the day. After all, it's not like it matters— what are they possibly going to do to me at this point if they catch me skipping my afternoon classes? Tell me I can't go to Brown?

The parking lot is strangely quiet, just a couple of birds chattering away in the trees and the occasional car cruising by out on the street. I unlock the car with shaking hands, jamming the key into the ignition and nearly clipping a red Passat as I peel out of the parking lot, everything

I should have said to Bex echoing meanly in my head. *I'm spoiled?* He's the one with his name on the auditorium at an Ivy League university. *I'm* responsible for what happened between us? He's the asshole who drove me to his fucking apartment.

Hot tears blur my view of the road in front of me. I head down Juniper Hill Avenue, midday traffic thinning out as I pass the municipal baseball fields and the golf course development, the function hall where we had my eighth-grade graduation party. I don't have any real destination in mind. I can't go home and face my parents. I can't turn around and go back to school. There's a part of me that wants to just keep on driving—to speed right out of this stupid town, to keep my foot pressed to the pedal until I get all the way to the Atlantic Ocean.

Finally I head for Sunrise without ever quite making the conscious decision to do it, instinct and muscle memory taking over. My gram is the only person I can imagine being around right now.

Camille is coming out of a suite down the hall as I step off the elevator, a blood-pressure cuff dangling from one hand. Her scrubs have rubber ducks parading across them today, her Crocs the same bright, cheery yellow.

"Marin," she says, looking surprised—and there's that

243

uncomfortable look again, that flicker of trepidation at the sight of me. "What are you doing here, hm? Shouldn't you be in school?"

"Reading day," I tell her, surprised at how smoothly the lie comes out of my mouth. "I just need to talk to my gram real quick."

Camille shakes her head. "It's not really a good time, sweetheart. You should come back later."

That surprises me—in all the years I've been coming here, Camille has never said anything like that to me before. "Why?" I ask, frowning. "What's going on?"

"She's having a tough day, that's all. She was a little agitated this morning. It's probably better if you just let her rest."

Camille's tone is light—friendly, even—but there's an underlying warning I've never heard from her before. "What do you mean, agitated?" I ask, trying to keep my own voice even. "Is she okay?"

Camille nods. "She's fine, sweetheart. She just—you know. Needs to take it easy until she's feeling more like herself."

"What, like she's not remembering stuff?" I shake my head. "That's okay though. I don't mind."

"Marin—"

"She knows who I am," I promise. "It's fine, Camille, honestly. I'll be quick."

Camille takes a step closer then—to try to block my path down the hallway, maybe, or to catch me by the arm—but I'm too quick and too determined and possibly a little too wound up, skirting past her and slipping down the brightly lit corridor to the door of Gram's suite. It's all the way closed today, which is unusual, but I knock lightly before pushing it open, same as always.

"Hi, Gram," I call, all slightly manic sunshine—then stop where I'm standing in the doorway, caught short. The woman sitting vacantly on the love seat doesn't look anything like my grandmother. She's not wearing any lipstick, her mouth so pale it's nearly vanished into the rest of her face. Her white hair is a matted mess. She's still in her pajamas, the undone top button revealing her sharp, jutting collarbones. Most of all she just looks *frail*.

"Who are you?" she asks, her blue eyes watery and suspicious.

I bite my lip. "Hey Gram," I say again, careful to keep my voice breezy. "It's me. Marin."

Gram shakes her head, stubborn. "I don't know you."

"I'm your granddaughter," I remind her, working hard to swallow down the sudden lump in my throat, knowing instinctively that getting emotional is only going to make this worse—which, I think bitterly, is something of a theme in my life lately. "I'm Dyana's daughter, remember?"

I take a step closer, but Gram holds her hands up, like the victim in an old murder mystery on the classics channel.

"Who? I don't *know* you," she repeats. "Where's the nurse?" Then, raising her voice toward the open door: "Hello! There's a strange woman in here! I need help!"

"Gram," I plead, "come on," but Camille is already here, laying a firm, gentle palm on my back.

"Well, hey there, Ms. Fran," she says calmly. "You're okay, I'm right here. I'm just going to take a stroll with our friend here, and then I'll be right back to get you some iced tea, how about?"

"I don't *know* her," Gram insists again—sounding more irritated than scared now, like I'm more inconvenience than threat. I don't actually know which one is worse.

I shouldn't have come here, I think dully. All I do is wreak disaster everywhere I go.

"I know," Camille says, wrapping an arm around my shoulders and squeezing once before steering me toward the door. "Come on, sweetheart."

"I'm sorry," I say once we're out in the hallway. "I'm sorry, I know you tried to tell me, I just—" *Thought I knew better*, I realize, feeling abruptly like an idiot on top of everything else. "I'm sorry."

"Marin, honey." Camille lets a breath out—not *mad* at me, exactly, but not as warm as she usually is either. "Why don't we call your mom, okay?"

Right away I shake my head. "It's fine, I'll just—I'll go. I'm sorry. You can go back in there and check on her. I didn't mean to make things worse."

"Marin—" Camille starts, and I know she's going to try to comfort me, even though it's not her job to do that. I hold my hands up to stop her, then turn and make a beeline for the stairs, tears aching at the back of my throat.

Down in the parking lot I sit in the car for a long time, wiping tears and snot and so much sadness from my face. I remember when I was a kid, before Gracie was born, even, when I used to stay with Gram overnight at her house in Brockton. It wasn't long after Grandpa Tony had died and she used to let me sleep in the big bed with her, the two of us watching reruns of nineties sitcoms while the AC unit hummed in the window. She used to pet my hair until I fell asleep.

Finally, exhausted, I pull out of the parking lot and head for home. The fastest route takes me back by school, and I glance over at the parking lot as I'm idling at the red light: eighth period got out a while ago, and the grounds are mostly empty. In fact, I realize with a quick, nasty jolt,

Mr. Beckett's Jeep is one of the only cars still parked in the lot. It's sitting there smugly under a blooming dogwood tree not far from the senior entrance, his stupid Bernie Sanders sticker fading on the bumper.

I think, very clearly: *Don't be such a good girl.*

That's when I turn into the lot.

I pull up beside the Jeep and yank the emergency brake, leaving the engine running while I pop the trunk and jump out onto the concrete. I haven't even really articulated a plan to myself when I grab the poster paint left over from the day of Elisa's volleyball game—still sitting in the trunk next to my mom's first aid kit and a couple of overdue library books, like deep in the back of my own secret brain I knew I might need it again. It feels like a relic from a totally different past.

I clamp a dry, crusted-over paintbrush in my teeth and twist the lid off the tub of paint with shaking hands, glancing over my shoulder to make sure no one is coming; the parking lot is deserted, even the birds have gone home for the day. It's like I'm totally outside myself as I scrawl the first word I can think of, the letters huge and red and dripping across Bex's back windshield. When I'm done I throw the rest of the paint at the car for good measure before standing back for a moment, admiring my handiwork.

Then I get back in my car and drive away.

THIRTY-TWO

I've barely made it through the door of my first-period French class the following morning when Madame Kemp nods in my direction.

"Marin," she says distractedly as she lopsidedly scrawls this morning's irregular verbs on the whiteboard, "there's a pass for you on my desk over there. Ms. Lynch says they want you down in the office."

I freeze where I'm standing, fingers curled tightly around the strap of my backpack. All at once I think of *Thelma & Louise*, this old movie my mom and I watched last year on cable about two friends who kill a guy in self-defense and then go on the run. The movie ends with the two of them driving into the Grand Canyon rather than giving themselves up to the police—this incredible, shocking freeze-frame of the car flying over the cliff that I couldn't get out of my head for weeks after I saw it. It was weirdly exhilarating, the idea of these two women refusing to engage with an unfair system. Looking at a menu of shitty choices and deciding to go out on their own terms.

Of course: we never saw the actual crash.

I shuffle down the senior stairs to the admin suite, where Ms. Lynch is diligently adding balloon emojis to the birthday wishes she's composing on someone's Facebook.

"Marin," says Mr. DioGuardi when I knock on the open door of his office, not bothering to say hello this time. I guess we're officially past formalities at this point. "Sit."

I plunk down obediently as Mr. DioGuardi pops his whistle into his mouth, the faintest, shrillest shriek filling the air every time he breathes. Finally he pulls it out again and eyes me across the desk. "So," he says, meaty hands folded. "Do you want to start, or should I?"

"Um," I say, not sure of the protocol here. In my entire life, I've never really gotten in trouble—and I'm pretty sure that's what's about to happen here, though I'm not sure who possibly could have seen me. "You can start."

I don't mean to sound sullen, exactly, but I can tell that's how Mr. DioGuardi takes it.

"All right," he says crisply. "Have it your way." He turns his computer monitor around so that it's facing me, hitting the space bar on the keyboard so the grainy security camera footage on the screen starts to move.

Yup, I think with surprising numbness, watching in silence as my car pulls up beside Bex's, as I hop out of the driver's seat and open my trunk. *Definitely about to get in trouble.*

I stare at the screen, transfixed by my yesterday-self as one by one the letters appear on the back of Bex's car: *S*, then *C*, then *U*, then the dark red curves of the *M*. It occurs to me, if I was going to get caught anyway, that I could have gone ahead and picked a longer word.

"What were you thinking?" Mr. DioGuardi asks, and I look at him, startled. For a second I almost forgot he was there. "Quite seriously, Marin, what on earth was going through your head?"

"Well," I say, truly considering it. "I wasn't thinking about the security cameras, I can tell you that much."

That's the wrong thing to say: Mr. DioGuardi glowers at me across the desk, his dark eyebrows nearly connecting. "Is this funny to you?" he demands.

"No," I promise immediately, and it's the truth. "I

don't think it's funny at all."

"Then I would be very careful how you handle this situation," he instructs me.

Clearly, I've exhausted his store of patience.

"Your future is in your hands right now. We're suspending you for two weeks, effective immediately. Unless you want to turn that into an expulsion—"

"I'm sorry, *what?*" I shove my chair back, jumping to my feet like I'm trying to escape a burning building. "You're—?"

"What did I *just* say, Marin?" Mr. DioGuardi's cheeks redden. "Lucky for you, Mr. Beckett has agreed not to press criminal charges."

I sit back down, not so much because he's telling me to as because I think my legs might actually give out underneath me.

"Um," I say again, wrapping my hands around the armrests in a pathetic attempt to ground myself. I can taste this morning's orange juice rising dangerously at the back of my throat. "Okay."

"He and I are both willing to acknowledge the emotional stress you've been under," Mr. DioGuardi continues, "and we understand the possibility that you weren't entirely yourself."

Not myself, I think dully, staring down at my hands like they're somehow completely separate from my body.

"The suspension is effective immediately," Mr. Dio-Guardi says again. "I'll be calling your parents to inform them of the situation, and Ms. Lynch can escort you to your locker to get your things."

"I don't need an escort," I tell him, forcing myself to my feet again. Nothing about this conversation seems real. *Suspended*. Me. He might as well be telling me he's sending me off to the moon.

"Marin—"

"I said I don't need one!" I snap, and it comes out a lot more like a wail than I mean for it to. Right away I hold my hands up in surrender, like a bank teller being held hostage. "I'm going, okay? I'm going."

Just for a moment Mr. DioGuardi looks at me with something like sympathy. "All right," he says quietly. "Go get your things, then."

The bell rings just as I stumble dazedly out of the admin suite, classroom doors slamming open like they're spring-loaded and the entire student body spilling out into the hallway. I almost crash right into Jacob, his immaculate Top-Siders gleaming white under the fluorescents and an against-dress-code Sox hat cocked on his head, not that anybody's going to say anything to him about it.

"Hey, Marin," he says, smiling a twisty, unpleasant smile. Then he nods at the admin office. "You making some alone time with DioGuardi now too?"

It's like something in me just breaks then, like everything I've been holding in with varying degrees of success in the last few months comes exploding out all at once. Before I even know I'm going to do it I'm lunging at him, shoving him as hard as I can in the chest and shoulders, the heels of my hands connecting with a satisfying thud. It's ridiculous—I'm emphatically not a fighter, Gracie and I never even pulled each other's hair as little kids—but Jacob's not expecting it; I shove him again, even harder this time, knocking him loudly into the bank of lockers behind him.

"What the fuck, Marin?" he yells, arms coming up to try and defend himself. "You're fucking insane!"

"And you're an asshole!" I can hear assorted gasps and shouts all around us, my vision blurred at the corners of my eyes. "And I've had it with letting you all just get away with saying shit like that!"

It's a spectacle, the exact kind of thing I've tried to avoid since I got back to school after break—hell, like I've tried to avoid my whole entire *life*. Maybe he's right. Maybe I am insane, hysterical, attention-hungry, desperate. Maybe I'm everything everyone thinks I am, but I can't bring myself to care. This whole little rebellion was a stupid idea to begin with.

And all at once I've got nothing left to lose.

I'm about to go after him again when Gray swoops in out of nowhere, dropping his crutches to the ground and wrapping his arms around my waist. "Let me go!" I order, trying to pry his arms off me. I don't want another guy touching me right now. I don't want anyone holding me back.

"Hey, hey, hey," Gray says, hauling me away from the crowd with a few choice words for the scrum of onlookers. He's twice my size, but I'm thrashing; I reach back and catch him on the side of his jaw before he finally deposits me in the hallway that leads to the library and nurse's office, quiet and dark in comparison to the rest of school.

"Let me *go*," I insist, though he's already done it, hobbling sideways on his walking cast, pain visible in the twist of his handsome features. The bell rings for the start of class, though it sounds strangely far away.

Gray shakes his head. "What *was* that?" he asks, bewildered. "Are you okay?"

"I'm fine," I snap, making to brush past him; he reaches for my arm, and I hiss. "Stop. Can you stop? I am so *sick* of this."

God, I have to get out of here. As soon as DioGuardi hears about this, I know I'm going to be facing an expulsion; I want to run as far as I can and never come back.

"Marin," Gray says, reaching for my hand again; I yank myself away, and he holds his palms out. "I'm sorry. I'm sorry, I just—"

"I said *stop*!" I tell him, my voice echoing down the hallway. "Stop trying to fix everything, or protect me, or whatever it is you think you're doing. Just leave me alone for once, okay?"

"Okay," Gray says, hands still up like I'm a wild animal—like maybe I'm dangerous, and need to be contained. "I won't touch you again, I promise. I'm sorry. But can you please just talk to me for a sec?"

I shake my head. I can't take his affable good-guy act right now—because let's be real, that's probably what it is, right?

"You're not helping," I inform him. "Nothing you've done this whole time has helped, actually, so—" I break off. I don't know why I'm saying this. Part of me doesn't know what I'm saying, but I can't stop.

"Look," I try again. "This has been fun. But I just don't think it's a good idea to keep—"

"To keep what?" Gray frowns. "What's not a good idea?"

"You and me."

"Seriously?" He looks baffled. "I don't—why? Because Jacob is a dick?"

I gape at him. "*That's* what you think this is about?"

"No, no," he amends quickly. "Of course not, but—"

"No." I cut him off. I'm just so done. We're so done. "It's over."

"I—"

"*No*," I say again—and there's something that feels satisfying about it, finally, even if there's a voice in my head that's already wondering if this is really the bridge I want to burn. His instructions from weeks ago come tumbling back to me then, and before I can stop myself I tell him: "With respect, Gray? Fuck off."

For a second Gray just stares at me, eyes flickering with recognition, and my heart breaks a little bit. Then his face falls.

"Yeah," he says, and his voice is so quiet. "I can do that."

THIRTY-THREE

I manage to make it home and get into bed without talking to anybody, pulling the covers up over my head and closing my eyes. I know Mr. DioGuardi is going to call here. It's only a matter of time.

Sure enough, when the knock on my door comes it's both of my parents, hands linked, their faces twin pictures of worry.

"So," my mom says. She sounds remarkably calm—calmer than I've heard her since this whole thing started, actually, her dark hair pulled neatly off her face. "Do you want to talk about it now, or do you want to talk about it later?"

"Later," I mumble into the pillows.

To my surprise, she nods.

"Okay," my dad says. "We love you."

That's when I start to cry.

Both of them are across the room in a second, like I'm a toddler who fell down learning to walk.

"Sweetheart," my dad says, while my mom sits down beside me on the mattress, "what the hell happened?"

I take a deep breath, the whole sad story spilling out of me all at once: the email from Brown and the call with Kalina, the visit with Gram, what I did to Bex's car.

"Everything you guys did. The SAT tutors. Those stupid piano lessons. Everything Gram wanted for me. I blew it all," I tell them.

My mom shakes her head. "You didn't blow anything."

"Really?" I ask tearfully. "Honestly, name one thing I haven't totally ruined in the last couple of months. Brown. My friendship with Chloe. Gray. And it's all my fault." I swipe at my face with the back of my hand, angry and embarrassed. "All of this is my fault."

"What?" My mom shakes her head, baffled. "No, sweetheart. That's not true. How could any of this possibly be your fault?"

"Because I had a crush on him!" It comes out like a

keen, high-pitched and humiliating. "I did! And I *did* hang around all the time, and it did give him the wrong idea, and—"

"Hold on a second," my mom says, wide-eyed. "No way. That's not how this works, okay? That's not how any of this works."

She shakes her head one more time. "Sweetheart, do you know how many people get crushes on their teachers? Do you know how many teachers *I* had crushes on, growing up?"

"It's not the same," I insist. "If I hadn't—"

"It's the teacher's job to set the boundary," my dad says firmly. "Because the teacher is the adult."

Logically, of course, I know they're right. Bex and I weren't equal partners in some doomed flirtation; he was the authority figure, and I was a kid in his class. But looking around at the total wreckage of my life right now, it's hard to make myself believe it.

"Still," I say—shrugging half-heartedly, unconvinced. "I should have known better."

"*He* should have known better." My mom puts her arms around me then, gathering me close and stroking a hand through my hair. "And he *did* know better. And all of this is so unfair."

On that last point, at least, it's difficult to argue, so instead I let her hold me, closing my eyes against a sudden wave of exhaustion.

"I hate him," I mutter into her neck.

"I know," my mom says, her grip tightening reassuringly. "I fucking hate him too."

THIRTY-FOUR

The first couple of days of my suspension aren't actually so terrible. I watch a bunch of low-budget rom-coms on Netflix. I take myself on a long, winding walk. I heft Gram's old *The Silver Palate Cookbook* off the shelf in the kitchen and fumble my way through the recipe for orange-pecan loaf, leave it on the counter for my mom to bring to her and the nurses in the morning.

That's when the boredom sets in.

I lie on my bed and stare at the ceiling for a while. I will myself not to check my phone. I'm contemplating cleaning out my closet—which is how you know I'm truly desperate—when I hear the doorbell chime downstairs.

"Marin, honey!" my mom calls a moment later, the faintest hitch of surprise just barely audible in her voice. "You've got company!"

I'm startled too: seriously, is there anybody in my entire life I haven't somehow alienated lately? I shuffle out into the hallway and down the steps, making it as far as the landing before I stop on the matted carpet. Chloe is standing in the foyer in a silky top and a pair of open-toed booties, hands shoved into the back pockets of her dark skinny jeans. Her eyeliner is as perfectly applied as always, but for the first time in a long, long time her lips are pale.

"What are you doing here?" I ask, but then I notice the hunch of her narrow shoulders like she's shielding herself from a blow, and some dormant best-friend instinct sputters creakily to life. "Are you okay?"

Chloe shrugs, squinting at the 3D sea-glass sculpture on the wall in the hallway instead of looking at me. "Can we talk?" she asks.

I glance from her to my mom, who's slipping discreetly into her office, then back to Chloe again. "Sure."

I pull a hoodie off the row of hooks next to the front door and we head outside to sit on the porch swing, the chain link groaning quietly as we rock back and forth. We've had almost every important conversation of our friendship out here: sixth grade, the two of us trying valiantly to decipher the primitive dick-and-balls cartoon Brandon Farrow had scribbled on the back cover of her notebook; freshman spring when she told me her sister was leaving college to do inpatient eating-disorder treatment; last year when I was deciding if I wanted to lose my virginity to Jacob. I used to think I could tell Chloe anything. But now I don't know what to say.

In the end it turns out I don't have to.

"Can I ask you a question?" she begins, picking at the polish on her freshly painted thumbnail. She still isn't looking at me. "Why did you trash Bex's car?"

I whirl around, shocked all over again. "*That's* what you came here to yell at me about?" I demand. "His douchey car? Because if it is you can just—"

"Can you calm down?" Chloe interrupts, finally turning to look at me. Her eyes are hot as flame. "I'm not yelling at you. Do you hear me yelling at you? I'm just asking you why you did it."

I shrug. "Why do you even care?"

Chloe huffs a breath out. "Marin," she says, tilting her head back against the swing. "Come on."

"You come on." I'm being a baby—I know I'm being a

baby—but I can't help it. I don't know how to not be hurt by what she did.

"Look." Chloe peels a flake of polish off her pinky nail, flicking it onto the floor of the porch. "I know I haven't been a very good friend to you lately—and I know that's even an understatement, probably," she says, holding a hand up when I let out a sound of protest. "And you don't owe me any kind of explanation. But I'm listening, if you want to tell me."

So: I tell her. I tell Chloe everything, from Bex's first day back to my call with Kalina, to his grip on my arm that day in the stairwell. "He wanted to get back at me for telling, and he did," I finish finally. "So I guess I just wanted to . . . get back at him too." I reach one foot out and push off the porch railing harder than I mean to, and we go swinging forward quickly. "But the only person I actually ruined anything for was myself."

The swing creaks back and forth, back and forth, and Chloe doesn't say anything. When I glance in her direction her face is almost as white as the clapboard on the front of the house.

"I'm sorry," she says, her eyes filling so suddenly with tears that I can't keep from gasping. "Marin. I'm so, so sorry."

Right away I shake my head. "Hey," I say, holding my hands up, palms out in shocked surrender. Our friendship has felt like one bizarre, inexplicable missed connection after another lately. But I wasn't prepared for this. "It's . . . okay."

"It's not!" she says, and she's up off the swing now, pacing across the porch. "It's a lot of things, Marin, but it is definitely not okay."

"Chloe," I say, curling my fingers around the edge of the porch swing. My voice is quiet. "What's going on?"

Chloe shakes her head, her eyes flicking to her car in the driveway like she can't decide if she wants to dive behind the wheel and peel away into the sunset or just take off on foot and never, ever stop. I know that look—I've seen it in the mirror a lot lately—but in the end she just sits back down beside me, clearing her throat like she's preparing to give testimony in a courtroom. She takes a deep breath.

"I thought he loved me," she confesses, then immediately digs the heels of her hands into her eye sockets, rubbing until her mascara smudges. "Oh my god, I can't believe I'm saying that out loud right now. I sound like a fucking idiot. I thought he *loved* me."

I shake my head. "Who?" I ask—even though I already know, in some secret part of my brain. Maybe I always did.

Chloe rubs her thumbs underneath her eyes, wiping the mascara away. "Who do you think?"

It started in October, she tells me. He took her to his apartment, in the Victorian house with the built-in bookshelves on either side of the fireplace. He wanted to lend her a book. They listened to records; he cooked her pasta. She told her parents she was at the library.

He told her she had an old soul.

"When you told me what happened between you guys I just kind of lost it," Chloe admits. "The way you described it, him being a creep—it didn't feel like that to me. Or not at the time, at least. I thought we were . . . a couple." She rolls her eyes and another tear slips down her cheek. "We did couple stuff. Like—I went with him to the Cape back in the fall."

My eyes widen. "You did what?"

"Can you not?" Chloe shakes her head. "I know now it was stupid."

"I don't think it's stupid," I promise. "I just—what, to a *hotel*?"

She shrugs. "His family has a house."

"Of course they do." I run my fingers through my hair. "I'm sorry. I'm being an asshole. I just—when?"

"The weekend I told you I was with Kyra."

"Oh my God, I *knew* there was no way you were voluntarily spending a weekend with her!" For a moment I'm weirdly, horribly vindicated—that I knew her that well, at least, that I wasn't totally fooled—and then I realize how messed up that is. "What did you tell your parents?" I ask.

"School trip," she says miserably. "I made a fake permission slip and everything."

"Weren't you worried I'd say something to them about it when I was at work?"

"Are you kidding me?" Chloe exhales sharply. "I was *terrified*. It was all I could think about all weekend, only I didn't want to tell him that, because I didn't want to remind him—"

"That you're *seventeen*?"

"All right!" Chloe explodes, shocking us both into silence for a moment. When she speaks again her voice is barely more than a whisper. "After you went to his apartment . . . he told me he'd just tried to be nice to you." Her nail polish is mostly gone by now, pale pink dust scattered across her lap. "Like, that it was this totally harmless thing, and you'd gotten the wrong idea, or whatever. But then he broke up with me."

"And that's why you were so pissed?"

Chloe nods. "He said it was too dangerous now, and I

blamed you," she admits. "I'm sorry, I know it's like I've never seen a movie or watched a TV show or read a book in my entire life, but I just . . . I did. I thought this was different, and I blamed you. I felt like you took him away from me."

"I get it," I say. "I mean, it sucks, but I do."

"And I hate telling you this, but then after a while, we started back up again, but it wasn't the same. *He* wasn't the same, and there was, like, this part of me that knew he was going to do something to you. I just . . . I should have been there for you," she says, voice breaking. "You're my best friend, and I was—you had to do all this stuff by yourself."

I shake my head, trying to push away the picture of everything she's telling me now. "I wasn't by myself," I promise her, thinking of my parents and the book club and Ms. Klein. Thinking, with a pang behind my rib cage, of Gray. "But I really did miss you."

"Yeah," Chloe says, wiping her face with a heel of her hand. "Me too."

We swing for a while, neither one of us saying anything. I look out at the late-winter street. Jayden next door is pushing a plastic shopping cart up and down the front path, determined; Mrs. Lancaster is salting her sidewalk three houses down.

"Do you think I should report him?" Chloe asks finally. "To Mr. DioGuardi, I mean?"

I shrug. "I don't know," I tell her. "You have to do what feels good to you, I guess. Or, like, not even good, necessarily—just, least bad. I mean, I thought reporting was the right thing in the moment, and maybe I still do. But honestly I don't know that if it was worth it, you know? Half the school still thinks I made it up."

I tell her about the process with DioGuardi and the school board and how that didn't work. How, no offense, but they'd probably make it into Chloe's fault. "I'm not saying you shouldn't do it. It's not my place at all. I just . . . I don't know. I wish I could say it would work."

Chloe thinks about that for a moment, brushing the nail polish crumbs carefully off her jeans. Then all at once her head pops up.

"You know what?" she asks, turning to me with something like a smile passing across her expression. "I think I've got a better idea."

LETTER FROM THE EDITORS:
THE WHOLE TRUTH
BY MARIN LOSPATO AND CHLOE NIARCHOS

Dear Fellow Students, Faculty, and Administration of Bridgewater Preparatory,

Over the past several weeks, many of you may have heard rumors regarding allegations against a much-beloved teacher here at Bridgewater. As a community, it's safe to say we have struggled to separate information from innuendo and reconcile our own personal experiences with others' lived realities. It is never easy to come to terms with the idea that someone we admire—even adore, even perhaps love—may not be worthy of our continued esteem.

However: as the coeditors of the Beacon and young journalists ourselves, we are committed to the integrity of this newspaper and to using its power to speak truth. We believe in the power of the press to bring about positive change in the communities it serves, and it is in this spirit of truth telling that we write to you today.

The allegations against this teacher—that he has had inappropriate emotional and physical relationships with his students; that he has invited students into his home under academic pretexts and made advances of a sexual nature;

that he has retaliated against students who have spoken up about his behavior—are true. We report this information with confidence in our sources, because our sources are each other. Both of us have experienced this teacher's behavior firsthand.

We trusted him. We looked up to him. We found him charming and charismatic. And he took advantage of us. We were not special. We were not, as he told us, "old souls." We were simply his students.

When one of us came forward with these allegations, Bridgewater Preparatory's official position was that the administration did not have enough credible information to pursue further disciplinary action against this teacher. When the other of us admitted her strikingly similar situation, we could not help but question if she would be met with the same response. Would she, too, be asked if she was simply "confused" by the situation? Would she suffer the same rumors? Would she, too, be accused of looking for attention?

We write this letter today to shine a light on a dark place at Bridgewater, and also in the hope that any other student who has had a similar encounter—be it with this particular teacher, another authority figure, or someone else at this school—will feel safe and supported should they choose to come forward.

We believe you.
Sincerely,
Marin + Chloe

THIRTY-FIVE

Our piece goes to print on the front page of the paper the following Monday, my first day back at school after suspension. I take care of the editing, double- and triple-checking our sources. Chloe somehow manages to keep the whole thing a secret from the rest of the staff, including, of course, Bex.

Newly unsuspended or not, there's no way I can sit through Bex's class this morning, so I head outside as the bell is ringing for the start of third period. It's almost spring now, the cold air laced with the smell of something damp and briny. I cross the muddy field and make my way up the bleachers, climbing halfway to the top before sitting down and tilting my head back toward the weak midday sunshine, like a new plant desperate to grow.

I don't know how long I'm sitting there, the light making patterns on the insides of my eyelids, before somebody calls my name from the other side of the field. I open my eyes and there's Gray crossing the fifty-yard line below me, backpack slung over one broad shoulder. He's off his crutches now but he's still walking with just the tiniest limp, the kind you wouldn't even notice if you hadn't spent the whole semester noticing things like the way he normally walks.

"Hey," I call back, holding up one hand in greeting as he makes his way carefully up the wide metal steps. He's wearing a Bridgewater hoodie over his uniform, his ridiculous step counter fastened securely around one wrist. "You back up to twenty thousand per day yet?"

"Getting there," he reports with half a smile. He hesitates a moment like he's asking for permission before I nod, and he settles himself down beside me, stretching his long legs out in front of him.

"I read your article," he says, nodding at the *Beacon* sticking out of his bookbag. "I think it's awesome. I mean, it's shit what happened to your friend Chloe, obviously, but . . . That was really brave of you guys."

I muster a smile. "Thanks." The truth is, it doesn't feel brave at all: I'm glad Chloe had the chance to talk about what Bex did to her. I'm a little nervous I'm going to get expelled. But mostly I'm just sort of numb. It's like I keep waiting for some cinematic moment to signal I'm totally over everything that happened, that means it's all done and dusted. But the hard, frustrating reality is that all I can do is move on one day at a time.

Both of us are quiet for a minute, watching as a couple of Canada geese totter across the field, honking irritably at each other. A chilly wind rustles the budding branches on the trees.

Finally Gray takes a breath. "I told my moms I don't want to go to St. Lawrence," he confesses.

"You *did*?" I whip around to look at him, everything that's happened between us momentarily forgotten. "How'd they take it?"

Gray shrugs. "I mean, they weren't thrilled," he admits. "They lawyered me pretty hard. But eventually we made a compromise—I can take the job at Harbor Beach as long as I'm also taking college classes someplace local, Bunker Hill or UMass or someplace. So I think I'm gonna do that."

"Good for you," I say, reaching out to squeeze his arm like a reflex before remembering myself and dropping my hand awkwardly. "I'm, um. Really proud of you."

"Thanks," he says, smiling a little sheepishly. "You're kind of the person who inspired me to do it, actually. I guess I figured if you could put yourself on the line, then at the very least I could nut up and tell my moms I didn't want to play sports at college."

I laugh, I can't help it, and then my face abruptly falls. "Gray, I'm really sorry." This time I do touch him, just the tips of my fingers against the sleeve of his shirt. "About like . . . everything. I was a total asshole to you, and you didn't deserve it at all."

Right away, Gray shakes his head. "Hey," he says, "don't even sweat it. You were going through a thing, you know?"

"I mean, I guess so," I say, unwilling to let myself off the hook quite so easily. "But that's not an excuse. You were a really, really good boyfriend, and I took a bunch of stuff out on you that wasn't actually your fault. And I'm sorry."

"Really, Marin, don't worry about it." Gray waves me off. "We had fun, right?"

"I—yeah." That stings a little—both the words themselves and his casual shrug as he says them; just like that, he's the guy I thought he was back in October, a vaguely douchey lacrosse bro only looking for a good time. I think it could have been more than just fun, whatever there was between us. I guess I thought it was. But I'm pretty sure I missed my chance now. "Yeah," I say again, brushing some imaginary lint off my jeans. "We had fun."

Gray nods, like he's glad that's all settled. "So, um, what about you?" he asks, clearing his throat. "You figure out where you're headed in the fall?"

"Amherst," I report, aiming for excited and mostly getting there—it's still an awesome school, even if it's not the one my gram went to, and I know I'm incredibly lucky to have the option at all. "Sent in my deposit yesterday, actually."

"You're going to be amazing wherever you go," Gray predicts easily, like it's just a given. "Amherst's not too far either."

I look over at him in surprise, not sure what he means— not too far from here? Or from him? The miracle of Gray was always how easy he was to talk to. But now it's like I don't know how.

"No," I agree finally, careful. "Not too far."

Gray smiles. For a second it feels like he's going to say something else, or maybe like I am—like there's unfinished business here and both of us can feel it. But the bell rings for the end of the period before either one of us can find the words.

"Shit, I've got a trig exam," Gray says, getting to his feet and reaching down for his backpack. "Take care of yourself, okay? With the article and everything I mean. I'll see you around."

"Yeah," I say. "I will." Then, suddenly: "Gray—"

"Hm?" He turns around. "What's up?"

I open my mouth, then close it again. Of everything I've lost in the last few months, somehow this feels like the worst.

"Nothing," I tell him finally. "You take care of yourself too."

THIRTY-SIX

School is strangely quiet the rest of the day. Chloe and I were fully prepared for a fallout of epic proportions—we even drafted emergency letters to our respective colleges in the event we were both expelled—but other than my conversation with Gray on the bleachers, no one says anything to me about it. I take a calc quiz. I sit with the book club at lunch. Even Michael Cyr leaves me alone.

On one hand it feels like a massive relief—that editorial was the riskiest thing I've ever written, and even though I might have been prepared to sacrifice what's left of my future, I wasn't exactly looking forward to the consequences.

On the other hand, it's hard not to feel a tiny bit disappointed too. Like, does seriously no one even care?

Chloe picks me up the following morning, the two of us listening to the latest episode of our favorite creepy podcast and taking the long way so we can swing by the Starbucks drive-through for iced coffees and slightly dry croissants. By the time we pull into the Bridgewater parking lot it almost feels like it did last fall before everything happened.

That is, until we actually get inside.

I've become something of an expert in gauging the energy in the south hallway the last few weeks, and this morning it definitely feels like something unusual is happening, that sharp electric bite in the air. Sean Campolo's gaze cuts in between us. Allie Chao whispers something behind her hand.

"Oh, what the hell is this?" I can't keep myself from muttering. It feels like my first day back after break all over again, right down to the icy feeling creeping down my backbone. I thought I was immune to this, to the shame of being singled out and stared at. I guess, even after all this time, I was wrong.

I'm about to bolt—directly to first period, or possibly right out the door again—but Chloe reaches down and hooks her elbow in mine.

"Relax," she says, with all the easy intuition of seven years of best friendship. Her voice is perfectly level. "Whatever happens, we're together, right?"

I force a nod. "Right," I manage, and to my surprise I do feel a tiny zing of confidence, my spine straightening the slightest bit. "We're together."

We head toward our lockers, gather our books; down the hall I can see a gaggle of book clubbers sprawled in the lounge outside the cafeteria, and as we weave through the crowded hallway in their direction, I can see that Elisa is grinning. Lydia lifts her chin in a nod.

"Okay, no, seriously," I murmur, quiet enough that only Chloe can hear me. "What the hell is this?"

Before she can reply I spy Principal DioGuardi coming down the hallway from the direction of the admin suite in a blue button-down so shiny it's nearly iridescent. He catches my eye and motions us over, popping his whistle into his mouth.

"Girls," he says, pulling it out again as we approach him. "Can I speak with you for a moment?"

I take a breath. "Mr. DioGuardi," I begin, just like we practiced in Chloe's bedroom, "Chloe and I are happy to discuss whatever concerns you had about this week's issue. But I should let you know that we looked at the organizational paperwork for the *Beacon* before we published, and it says very clearly that the administration shall not interfere with the editorial page unless there's an egregious violation of—"

Mr. DioGuardi shakes his head. "It's not about that," he tells me. "Or it is about that, but—" He jams the whistle back into his mouth, looking visibly pained. "I just wanted to let you both know that Mr. Beckett has been removed from the faculty."

For a second I just blink at him dumbly. That is . . . not what I was expecting him to say.

"Really?" I blurt.

Mr. DioGuardi nods. "Other students have already come forward," he explains miserably. He looks exhausted, greenish bags under his eyes and a day's worth of beard on his chin; if things had gone a little bit differently between us, I'd almost feel sorry for him. "It seems there was . . . well. More of a problem with Mr. Beckett than we realized, certainly. Both here and at the last school he worked at."

The last school he worked at. I remember the first day Bex drove me home, that line about cooking dinner for students in his apartment and can't keep from shaking my head.

"He's really gone?" I ask, still looking for the catch somewhere, but Mr. DioGuardi nods again.

"Effective immediately," he reassures me. "He won't be back."

"Wow." It's more than I ever dreamed would happen, honestly. "That's . . . wow."

Chloe seems to consider that for a moment; to my surprise, she doesn't actually look satisfied. "So, Mr. Dio-Guardi," she says politely, cocking her head to the side, her eyes sharp and keen behind her glasses. "It sounds like what you're saying is that you were wrong not to believe Marin when she came to you in the first place, hm?"

Mr. DioGuardi frowns. "Well, it wasn't a question of belief or not," he explains, his gaze cutting from her to me and back again. "The board was working with the information they had at the time——"

"Including the information she gave you, right?"

"I . . . yes," Mr. DioGuardi admits. "But without corroborating——"

"So it almost kind of feels like you owe her an apology."

For a moment Mr. DioGuardi looks like he's going to argue, but in the end he just sort of sags.

"I'm sorry, Marin," he says, the words as stiff and awkward in his mouth as if he's trying to speak Klingon. "I know you've been through a lot these last couple of months."

It's not exactly stellar, as far as apologies go, and it turns out that I don't actually give a shit if he's sorry or he's not. I told the truth. Bex is gone. And Chloe and I are friends again. All told, I could have done worse. "Thanks," I say, cool as a glass of my gram's iced tea on the hottest day of summer. "I appreciate that."

Once he's gone I look around the hallway, then back at Chloe. Her expression is a shocked, delighted mirror of my own. "You wanna skip first period and go to the diner for breakfast?" I ask her. "Just you and me?"

"You know," Chloe says thoughtfully, "I think that is the best idea I've heard all year."

We link arms again and head back out into the parking lot. The sun is warm on the back of my neck.

THIRTY-SEVEN

I go by Sunrise after school on Friday and find Camille standing at the nurses' station, humming quietly to herself while she fills out some paperwork. Her Crocs are hot pink today, her scrubs printed with toucans and flamingos. An enormous Dunkin' iced coffee sweats at her side.

"I've got something for you," I tell her, digging around in my backpack for a moment before pulling out an Amherst T-shirt.

Camille's mouth drops open. "Oh, Marin, you didn't have to do that!"

"A promise is a promise," I say with a shrug. "I'm just

sorry it's not from Brown."

"Are you kidding?" she says. Her grin is wide and white. "I'm so proud of you, honey." She raises her eyebrows. "Are you proud of yourself?"

I consider that for a moment. "You know," I say finally, "I actually really am."

"Good," Camille says, reaching out and squeezing my shoulder before nodding down the hallway toward Gram's suite. "Let me know if you need anything, okay? She had a pretty good morning, but just in case."

I nod. It's the first time I've been back here on my own since the day Gram didn't recognize me—Mom and I went together one morning, and Gracie tagged along with me the time after that—and I can feel my heart thumping unpleasantly as I make my way down the hallway.

It's just Gram, I remind myself firmly. *Whether she remembers you or not, it doesn't change who she is to you.*

"Hey there," I say, knocking lightly on the door.

"Hi, Marin-girl."

I let a breath out, relief coursing through me at the sound of my own name. Gram is sitting on the love seat with a biography of Katharine Graham in her lap. She's wearing a linen shift dress and a pale pink cardigan, her hair pulled into a wispy knot at the base of her neck. The line of her lipstick is a tiny bit wobbly, but otherwise she looks like herself.

"Dad made a ciambellone," I tell her once I've kissed her hello, hefting the Tupperware carrier up as evidence. It's an Italian tea cake that she used to make when I was a kid, lemony and dense. I remember wandering around her yard with a hunk of it in my fist, Grandpa Tony's toy poodle Lola trying to nibble bits of it out from in between my fingers. "He used your recipe, so he said he wants your honest opinion about how it turned out."

"Oh, that's lovely!" she says, sounding genuinely pleased. "I got that recipe from my mother-in-law, did I ever tell you that? She was not a nice lady, your great-grandmother, but the woman knew her way around a kitchen."

I laugh, cutting us both slices and bringing them over to the coffee table, running my thumb over the edge of the delicate scalloped plate. "You got a crossword around here anywhere?" I ask. "I've been practicing."

We pass the better part of our visit that way, filling in the puzzle and catching up on my last few weeks of school. I'm telling her about the dress I got for spring formal when something about her expression, a wary uneasiness, stops me. "Everything okay?" I ask.

Gram nods. "You know," she says, and it sounds almost like an accusation, "I used to make a cake just like this."

I bite my lip, trying to keep my face neutral. "I know, Gram," I say gently. "It's your recipe, remember?"

She narrows her eyes then, and I know all at once that I've lost her.

"It's delicious, isn't it?" I ask, instead of trying to get her to remember. It's better not to push her when she gets like this, Mom explained after that last disastrous solo visit; she'll come back on her own when she's ready. It might be this afternoon, or it might not be. At some point she might not come back at all. "It tastes like spring."

I spend the rest of my visit chattering on, cheerful, keeping my voice light and full of air: about summer finally coming and the tulip beds in front of Sunrise; about Katharine Graham, who I know from Ms. Klein was the first female publisher of a major American newspaper. Gram, for her part, seems content to listen to me, nibbling at her cake and nodding politely at appropriate breaks in my monologue like I'm a particularly gregarious stranger in a train station. As I'm getting up to leave, she touches my hand.

"I like you," she says, her smile warm but somehow completely unfamiliar. "You remind me of myself."

I tilt my head to the side, swallowing hard. "I do?"

Gram nods. "You're a good girl," she continues, "but you don't always have to be *so* good." Then she raises her eyebrows, mischievous. "Lord knows I wasn't."

For a second she looks like herself again, Gram who bought me my first journal and grew prize-winning roses and taught me to separate eggs over her immaculately polished stainless steel sink; then she blinks and it's gone. I turn my hand over and squeeze hers for a moment, just gently, before letting go.

"I know," I promise. "I'll remember."

EPILOGUE

The year's final meeting of the feminist book club is on a warm Thursday afternoon at the beginning of June, a breeze blowing in through the open windows of Ms. Klein's classroom and the trees exploding into verdant green outside. Elisa's mom sends homemade tamales. Grace and I baked seven-layer bars. We read Warsan Shire's *Teaching My Mother How to Give Birth*, which was Lydia's pick—and which comes with the benefit of letting us watch Beyoncé's *Lemonade*, which is playing on a loop on a laptop at one corner of the room. Maddie and Bridget have an impromptu dance party going in one corner of the classroom, and I catch Dave singing along to "Formation" under his breath when he thinks no one is paying attention.

"You did something really good here, Marin," Ms. Klein says quietly, coming to stand beside me with a paper cup of seltzer in one hand. The club is going to keep meeting next year, the underclassmen decided; Lydia nominated Elisa to be president, and she ran unopposed. I like the idea of the club continuing on without me—it's dumb, maybe, but it kind of makes me feel like I'll have a real legacy at Bridgewater beyond just being the girl who got Bex fired.

Of course, I'm not mad if that's part of my legacy too.

The town paper ended up running a huge article on Bex, and Bridgewater caught a lot of heat for how they handled the whole situation. People were shocked by the administration's actions—or lack thereof.

"How could something like this still happen today?" everyone said—but I guess that's the reality, right? It does still happen. My mom kept threatening to call that lawyer, but in the end knowing the article was out there and Bex couldn't just could turn around and do the same thing at a different school felt like enough for me. All I wanted to do was move on.

Now I look around the classroom, my chest warm. Even Chloe came today, though she hadn't read the book.

"Are you sure it's okay?" she asked on the way over here, hesitating in the hallway. "To be crashing?"

"It's not really about the book," I promised, reaching for her hand and pulling her into the classroom. "I mean, it is and it isn't." Now I see her chatting with Elisa about the makeup artist who works on all Beyoncé's videos, and I can tell she's glad she came.

The only person who's missing is Gray.

I sigh, smiling half-heartedly at Ms. Klein before drifting over to the food table. I thought he might show up for nostalgia's sake—it's our last meeting, after all—but I guess I chased him away for good. And sure, I apologized that day on the bleachers. But I know better than most people that sometimes an apology isn't enough.

I'm just about to drown my sorrows in another tamale when I sense a movement behind me in the doorway; I turn around and there he is in his uniform and a Sox cap, smile as sheepish and crooked as the first day he joined the club. He catches my eye and grins.

I smile back, wide and honest.

It occurs to me that our story, whatever it might turn out to be, is far from over.

"Sorry I'm late," he says, shrugging a little shyly. "I needed to finish the book."

ABOUT THE AUTHORS

Candace Bushnell is the critically acclaimed *New York Times* bestselling author of *The Carrie Diaries*, *Sex and the City*, *Is There Still Sex in the City?*, *Lipstick Jungle*, *One Fifth Avenue*, *4 Blondes*, *Trading Up*, and *Summer and the City*, which have sold millions of copies. *Sex and the City* was the basis for the HBO hit shows and films, and its prequel, *The Carrie Diaries*, was the basis of the CW television show of the same name. *Lipstick Jungle* became a popular television show on NBC. *Is There Still Sex in the City?* is in development with Paramount Television. Candace lives in New York City and Sag Harbor.

Visit her at www.candacebushnell.com.

Katie Cotugno is the *New York Times* bestselling author of *Top Ten*, *99 Days*, *9 Days and 9 Nights*, *Fireworks*, and *How to Love*. She studied writing, literature, and publishing at Emerson College and received her MFA in fiction at Lesley University. Katie is a Pushcart Prize nominee whose work has appeared in *Iowa Review*, *Mississippi Review*, and *Argestes*, among others. She lives in Boston.

Visit her at ww.katiecotugno.com.